Flying the Dragon

Flying the Dragon

Natalie Dias Lorenzi

ini Charlesbridge

To all the Hiroshis and Skyes who have ever walked through my classroom door. Your courage and resilience never cease to amaze me.

The Japanese characters at the beginning of each chapter are the *kanji* for Hiroshi's and Skye's names.

First paperback edition 2014
Copyright © 2012 by Natalie Dias Lorenzi
Jacket and chapter decoration illustrations © 2012 by Kelly Murphy

Published by Charlesbridge, 85 Main Street, Watertown, MA 02472
(617) 926-0329 • www.charlesbridge.com

Library of Congress Cataloging-in-Publication Data
Lorenzi, Natalie Dias.
    Flying the dragon / Natalie Dias Lorenzi.
        p. cm.
    Summary: When Skye's cousin Hiroshi and his family move to Virginia from Japan, the cultural differences lead to misunderstandings and both children are unhappy at the changes in their lives—will flying the dragon kite finally bring them together?
    ISBN 978-1-58089-434-0 (reinforced for library use)
    ISBN 978-1-58089-435-7 (soft cover)
    ISBN 978-1-60734-529-9 (ebook)
    ISBN 978-1-60734-449-0 (ebook pdf)
1. Japanese American families—Juvenile fiction. 2. Moving, Household—Juvenile fiction. 3. Japanese—Virginia—Juvenile fiction. 4. Culture shock—Juvenile fiction. 5. Cousins—Juvenile fiction. 6. Kites—Juvenile fiction. 7. Schools—Juvenile fiction. 8. Virginia—Juvenile fiction. [1. Japanese Americans—Fiction. 2. Family life—Virginia—Fiction. 3. Racially mixed people—Fiction. 4. Moving, Household—Fiction. 5. Japanese—United States—Fiction. 6. Culture shock—Fiction. 7. Cousins—Fiction. 8. Kites—Fiction. 9. Schools—Fiction. 10. Virginia—Fiction.] I. Title.
PZ7.L885Fl 2012
813.6—dc23   2011033620

Printed in the United States of America
(hc) 10 9 8 7 6 5 4 3
(sc) 10 9 8 7 6 5 4 3 2

Display type set in Kid Captain and text type set in Adobe Caslon
Color separations by KHL ChromaGraphics, Singapore
Printed and bound by Worzalla Publishing Company in
    Stevens Point, Wisconsin, USA
Production supervision by Brian G. Walker
Designed by Susan Mallory Sherman

Skye had known something was coming. The way her dad had been acting lately was beyond his normal weirdness. She just never guessed the something coming would be a bunch of Japanese relatives she'd never met.

The first sign of trouble was when her dad switched from silverware to chopsticks. Maybe she shouldn't have been surprised. After all, her dad was Japanese. Sort of. He'd been born and raised in Japan but hadn't been back since he married her mom. To Skye he was pretty much American. And since Virginia is about as far away from Japan as you can get, Skye didn't blame herself for forgetting that she was half Japanese herself.

But it wasn't the chopsticks themselves that had started the whole thing. No, it happened when Skye had *asked* about them. Everything snowballed from there.

"What are you doing, Dad?" Skye's fork hovered above her spaghetti and meatballs.

Her dad leaned over his plate, two strands of slippery spaghetti trapped in his chopsticks. He winked at Skye, slurped the noodles into his mouth, and chewed, apparently oblivious to the trail of sauce left behind on his chin.

"I'm eating. What does it look like I'm doing?"

From the glint in his eyes, Skye figured he was up to one of his usual jokes.

Her mom handed him a napkin. "Your chin, honey."

He laughed. "Can you believe how rusty I am? Twelve years in America and I've forgotten how to eat."

Her mom laughed, too. "I never did get the hang of eating with chopsticks."

Neither had Skye. Come to think of it, Skye had never seen her mom use chopsticks. "Didn't you learn when you lived in Tokyo?"

Her mom shook her head. "Not even then. But it wasn't for lack of trying." She looked at Skye's dad and smiled. "Remember when you bought me a set of kids' chopsticks—with the ridges at the tips that make them easier to use? Supposedly."

Skye's dad nodded, grinning through a mouthful of spaghetti. "You wanted to become an expert before I took you . . . home." He lowered his chopsticks and set them on the table, their tips propped on a miniature, black lacquered wood version of a samurai sword.

Her mom stared at her fork as she trailed the pasta around her plate.

"What?" Skye took another bite. "So what happened? Did you learn how to eat with chopsticks?"

"Don't talk with your mouth full, Skye." Her mom set her fork down.

Skye swallowed in one gulp. "Okay, so what happened, then?"

Skye's parents had never talked much about her dad's family. She knew they lived in Japan and that her dad had three brothers and a father—Skye's grandfather. Her grandmother had died before Skye was born. She'd always wondered about her Japanese relatives, but after years of unanswered questions, she'd given up.

Tonight was no different. Her mom's chair scraped against the tile floor as she stood and brought her half-full plate to the sink. Her dad glanced once more at the chopsticks, picked up his fork, and finished his spaghetti in silence.

A week after the Chopsticks Incident came the *Itadakimasu* Disaster.

Skye and her parents went out for pizza with her soccer team to celebrate their win against the West Springfield Sprinters. But it wasn't the same without Lucy there. Skye's best friend had moved away a month before, all the way to San Francisco. That afternoon Skye had scored the winning goal without Lucy. When All-Star Amber had kicked the ball right to Skye in a smooth, perfect pass, Skye had thwacked it into the net. And to finish off a perfect afternoon, Coach Tess had announced the All-Star list for the coming summer.

Skye's name was finally on it.

Amber had been the team's top player since forever—and now here she was at the pizzeria chatting away with Skye about All-Star summer camp and coaches and plays. It should have been Skye's shining moment.

When the pizza arrived, everyone grabbed a slice, and that's when it happened. Skye's dad called out, "*Itadakimasu!*"

In front of everyone. He smiled as he said it, as if everyone at the table understood Japanese. *What is he doing?* Whenever Skye's dad spoke to her in Japanese, it was always at home or when they were alone. Never in front of a crowd.

3

Amber paused mid-bite, a tightrope of cheese stretching from her teeth to the tip of her pizza slice. She exchanged a look across the table with Kelsey. Skye thought it might have been a smirk, but it was hard to tell with their mouths full. Kelsey looked at Skye's dad and cocked her head. "What is that—Chinese?"

Skye wanted to roll her eyes. Japanese and Chinese sounded nothing alike.

Coach Tess laughed and asked, "Does that mean you like the pizza?"

That was all the fuel Skye's dad needed. "It means *enjoy your meal.*" From his wide grin Skye could tell he was loving every moment. Skye glanced at Amber and Kelsey, who were trying—and failing—to muffle a shared giggle.

Skye's mom chimed in. "It's Japanese, Kelsey."

"How do you say it, again?" Coach Tess leaned in from her seat at the head of the table. Everyone stopped talking and stared at her dad, but Skye kept chewing. Looking down and chewing.

"*Ee-tah-da-kee-mahs,*" her dad said, drawing it out. Coach Tess repeated the word and was rewarded with a bow from Skye's dad.

Just. Great.

Skye's mom beamed, like she had the most clever husband in the world. Coach Tess was smiling, but it looked to Skye like one of those polite, oh-isn't-that-(not)-interesting smiles. Kelsey and Amber didn't muffle their giggles this time. Skye told herself she didn't care that Amber and Kelsey were laughing at her dad—even though she wanted to give his shin a penalty kick under the table. Her dad just sat there, eating and grinning, totally clueless.

But that wasn't the end of it.

When everyone had finished their pizza, Skye's dad turned to her and said, "*Gochisou sama deshita,*" with a satisfied pat of his stomach. Skye nodded without looking up from her plate. *Okay, so you enjoyed the meal. Would it kill you to say it in English?*

When they were finally back in the car, Skye couldn't hold it in any longer. "Dad?" She took a breath to keep herself from shouting. "Why were you speaking Japanese in there?"

He kept his eyes on the road. Whenever her dad didn't answer right away, it meant he was thinking, and there was no use hurrying him. Tonight was no exception.

Her mom sighed. "We need to tell her, Issei."

"Tell me what?"

Her dad glanced at Skye in the rearview mirror, then looked away.

"Issei," her mom said, her voice soft.

Skye's dad nodded, eyes still on the road. "I've been thinking lately that you and I should speak in Japanese more often, *ne?*"

Skye frowned. "But we do."

"Not as much as we used to. And whenever I speak to you in Japanese, you answer in English."

Her mom turned and looked at Skye. "This is my fault, really. I should study more so you two don't have to stick to English around me." Even after she'd lived in Tokyo for two years, her mom's Japanese had never been great.

They pulled into the driveway. The conversation seemed closed, but Skye knew there had to be more. She'd had enough of secrets.

"Be careful, Hiroshi. That kite is too close to the dragon."

"I see it, Grandfather." The winter wind skipped off Tachibana Bay, whipping Hiroshi's hair in all directions at once. Hiroshi steered the dragon kite out of danger with a simple tug of his line. His eyes tracked the dragon now as it nibbled at the sky, swooping among the other villagers' kites.

"It's perfect, Grandfather." Hiroshi beamed.

"We still have a month to make any changes," Grandfather said with a nod. "But it's flying well." Grandfather closed one eye against the sun. "There are many fine kites up there on the wind. You must not let them distract you. Remember to focus on—"

"The line, not the kite. Don't worry, Grandfather—I'll remember."

Hiroshi had dreamed of this year's *rokkaku* kite battle ever since he was old enough to remember his dreams. Now that he was eleven, he could finally enter the competition on his own. Kites would knock each other from the sky. Lines would slice other lines, as kites and dreams fell to the ground like stones. The lucky ones would float back to earth, cradled in the cupped hands of a gentle breeze. The unlucky ones would crash, splintering into a hundred pieces. Only one kite would remain. Hiroshi prayed it would be his. A member of the Tsuki family had always won the master flier title ever since Grandfather had first entered as a boy. Hiroshi couldn't disappoint his family. He had to win.

"How do you think the battle will turn out, Grandfather?"

The wind gusted, and Grandfather zipped up his jacket. "Do not fill your head with thoughts of winning or losing. You need to empty your mind and listen to what the wind and the kite are telling you."

Hiroshi pulled in the line then released it, urging the dragon to climb higher and higher. The wind rushed past his ears, but it wasn't telling him anything. The only voices he heard belonged to the seagulls, who scolded the kites for invading their patch of sky.

Hiroshi frowned. "But what if I can't hear what the kite and the wind are saying?"

"You will," Grandfather said. "You will."

Hiroshi wasn't so sure. Maybe Grandfather should fly the kite this year, and Hiroshi could be his assistant again.

"Your time has come, Hiroshi. You are ready." Grandfather chuckled. "It is time I became your assistant, wouldn't you say? I will keep track of the extra line, and you will concentrate on flying."

Hiroshi nodded. He wanted to shield his eyes from the sun, but that would mean letting go of the line with one hand; he needed both hands to avoid the other kites. He would not dishonor Grandfather by crashing the dragon kite before the battle.

Hiroshi remembered with a shiver what had happened last year to Yuki, the mayor's daughter. In the last few minutes of the battle, a gust of wind had sent Yuki's kite into a downward spiral. In desperation, she had reeled in some line—an amateur move. She should have given the line more slack. The kite dove straight into the ground, leaving months of meticulous work in scattered pieces on the grass.

Hiroshi blinked away the memory. He wouldn't let that happen to him. The wind swirled harder, and he struggled to tame the dragon.

Grandfather placed his hand on Hiroshi's shoulder. "Time to bring the kite in."

"Are you sure? I can keep going." Hiroshi's arms burned, but he'd never admit that to Grandfather.

"The wind is getting too strong. Better to stop for today."

One by one the villagers coaxed their reluctant kites lower and lower. The kites flapped wildly in protest until they hung low enough to pluck from the air.

As Hiroshi rolled up his line, he heard the mayor's voice behind him. "Will you be giving the rest of us a chance at the title this year?"

Hiroshi spun around to face the mayor and bowed, his body hinged at the waist, hands at his sides.

"With a master kite maker and *rokkaku* champion for a grandfather, surely Hiroshi will have an advantage," the mayor said, smiling.

Grandfather snuck a wink at Hiroshi. "Our Hiroshi constructed this kite himself. He will bring honor to our family, no matter the outcome."

Hiroshi tried stuffing his pride back down inside his heart, but it didn't work. It bubbled up and spilled over into a smile that tugged at the corners of his mouth. He looked at the ground and hoped the mayor hadn't noticed.

Hiroshi knew he was expected to show his *aiso warai*, the pretend smile grown-ups sometimes wore to hide their true feelings. His expression should show his embarrassment at such a high compliment. But he couldn't do it. Hiroshi wasn't embarrassed by Grandfather's words; he was proud. If he looked at the mayor now, he would surely give away his *honne*—his true feelings.

"Some of us have made our kites with carbon tubes and nylon this year," the mayor said. "Much stronger than bamboo and *washi* paper. Perhaps this will prove to be an advantage over those who still make their kites the old-fashioned way."

"Perhaps," Grandfather said. "It does present a challenge for those who still follow tradition." He put his hand on Hiroshi's shoulder. "We welcome the challenge. Good luck to you and your family in this year's battle."

The mayor walked away. When Grandfather bent to gather the line and reel, he whispered, "They'll need luck." Hiroshi laughed.

"Come on, Grandfather! Mother's making *yakisoba* for lunch."

Grandfather smiled. "You go ahead. I need to stop by the workshop first."

As Hiroshi sprinted through the village, he wished Grandfather were racing alongside him, like he used to. Grandfather tired easily these days.

Hiroshi's stomach rumbled when he thought of the tender pork and noodles awaiting him. He burst through the door and hopped from one foot to the other, pulling off his shoes. The nutty scent of *yakisoba* sauce drew him into the house, where he found his parents already at the table. But when he saw Father's frown and Mother's eyes glistening with tears, Hiroshi's smile faded.

Skye

"So what's the something you need to tell me?" Skye stood with her hands on her hips.

Her parents exchanged nervous looks. "I told you," her dad began. "You and I need to speak in Japanese more often."

Skye shook her head. "It's more than that, and you're just not telling me. You never tell me anything."

Her dad sighed. "Let's go sit down." He turned toward the living room.

Part of her wanted to run past him and sit down—the part that was dying to finally know the family secret. The other part wanted to drag her feet—because maybe this secret was something she didn't want to know.

Her mom and dad sat on the couch, but Skye felt too jumpy to sit. Her parents looked like they didn't know what to say, so Skye blurted out, "Why were you acting all Japanese at the pizzeria? Everybody was staring."

Now her dad looked angry. No, sad. Maybe something in between. "Acting Japanese? I am Japanese, Skye."

If it weren't for the hurt look on his face, Skye would have laughed. "Yeah, but you're mostly American now, right?"

Her mom looked miserable. "Skye, your dad gave up a lot of things when we were married." She took Skye's hand and guided

10

her to a spot on the couch between them. "He has sacrificed so much for us, and now we need to help him. His family will be coming here."

"What?" Skye blinked.

Her dad cleared his throat, looking like he'd rather eat live squid than say whatever he was about to say. "Skye, my father is coming here, to Virginia. With my brother, his wife, and their son, Hiroshi."

All these years knowing almost nothing about her Japanese relatives, and now they were coming? Here? "How long will they be visiting?"

Another glance between her parents, then her mom answered. "They'll be living here."

"With us?"

"No. We've found a house they'll be renting here in the neighborhood."

So why did her parents look so down about the whole thing? Skye had always suspected there'd been some kind of family argument back when her parents got married. *Wasn't it about time they all made up?*

"That's why I want us to speak in Japanese more," her dad said, "so you can talk to your grandfather, aunt, and cousin. Your uncle already speaks English."

Right. That made sense, then. Although Skye understood whatever her dad said in Japanese, answering him was just easier in English. But she could try. "Okay, then. I'll speak in Japanese more."

Her parents still didn't look thrilled. Her dad let out a slow breath. "Skye, speaking with me in the evenings and on weekends

11

is not enough. I've signed you up for Saturday Japanese school."

"School? On Saturdays?" Skye shook her head. "But what about soccer?"

"You can still finish out this season," her mom said. "The current Japanese session won't interfere with spring soccer." Skye relaxed. "But with the summer session—" Her mom sighed. "I'm sorry, honey. I'm afraid you won't have time for the All-Star team."

"What?" Skye stared at her mom. *This can't be happening.*

Her mom squeezed Skye's hand. "I know how much the team means to you, Skye. But we've checked into every school in the DC area, and the summer classes you'd qualify for are in the mornings."

"The classes I qualify for? What's that supposed to mean?"

"Beginner and intermediate classes are in the mornings," her dad said. "Only advanced classes are in the afternoons."

"But I'm advanced. I understand Japanese."

"It's not enough, Skye." He shook his head. "Your spoken Japanese is not advanced."

Skye snatched her hand away from her mom's and stood, tears already forming. "I won't go, then. I've waited forever to make the All-Star team, and I'm not going to miss it for a bunch of stupid lessons. I can speak enough Japanese to get by."

Her dad stood, too. "You need to learn more. To get to know your relatives."

"But they're moving here! I'll have plenty of time to get to know them."

Her dad looked sadder than she'd ever seen him. "You don't have plenty of time, Skye." He turned to go, and then stopped. Without looking back, he said, "You're going to the Japanese

12

Saturday school. And that's final." He strode from the room and out onto the back deck.

Skye fought to stay calm. Her mom could smooth things over. She wouldn't really make Skye do this. Would she?

Her mom shrugged. "I'm sorry, honey. But your dad is right." When Skye opened her mouth to protest, her mom held up her hand. "Wait, Skye. I know this is hard for you. But the reason the family is coming is because your dad's father—your grandfather— is sick."

Skye's anger cooled, but only by a few degrees. "He's coming here to get better?" Her mom hesitated, then nodded. Skye shrugged. "Okay, so he'll come here, get better, and I'll play on the All-Star team. I don't see what the big deal is."

Skye's mom took her hands. "The director of the Japanese school has agreed to let you enroll in the intermediate class mid-semester, starting now. There will be several exams at the end of this semester that will determine whether or not you'll go on to the advanced class this summer. If not . . ."

"If not what? I can pass the exams."

Her mom looked doubtful. "Skye, I don't want you to set your-self up for disappointment. You can try out for All-Stars again next year and every year after that, if you want to. Your dad's right. You need to do this."

Skye couldn't believe it—wouldn't believe it. She sprinted out of the room, flew up the stairs, and slammed her bedroom door. But she didn't cry. There was no need to cry: she was going to play on that All-Star team. No matter what.

"Come sit with us, Hiroshi," Father said.

Hiroshi sat, looking from one parent to the other. "What is it?"

Mother glanced at Father, then nodded once. Father cleared his throat. "Hiroshi, we have something to tell you." Whatever it was, the news couldn't be good. Hiroshi forgot about being hungry.

Father rested his hands on either side of his plate. "Do you remember the business trip I took last month?"

"Yes, I remember." Father had brought Hiroshi a snow globe of the US Capitol in Washington, DC.

Father paused, the lines in his forehead deepening. "I've received a job offer. We're moving."

Hiroshi blinked. For a moment he stopped breathing. "W-what do you mean? Where? When?"

"Your father has accepted a job in Washington. Grandfather will be coming with us, of course."

Father placed his hand over Mother's. "I've found a furnished house that we'll be renting for the first year. I'll need to report to work next month."

"The *first* year? Next month?" A million thoughts tumbled through Hiroshi's head like stringless kites in a storm. "But the kite battle is next month. I can't miss it!"

"I'm sorry, Hiroshi. But it's for the best," Father said.

Hiroshi gripped the edge of the table to steady himself. "For the best? Not for me. Not for Grandfather—he'd never leave Japan!" He searched his parents' faces. Mother lowered her head, but not before Hiroshi saw a tear slide down her cheek.

"That's enough, Hiroshi. You're upsetting your mother."

Hiroshi bowed his head. The plate of *yakisoba* noodles in front of him turned his stomach. He had to get out of there. He scrambled to his feet and ran out the door.

"Your shoes!" called Mother, but Hiroshi left her words behind.

The gravel on the road stung Hiroshi's feet, but he didn't care. He raced down the lane, past Yakura-san's fruit and vegetable stand, past Taiko-san's dry cleaning store, past the *sento*—the public bathhouse, where men entered carrying plastic buckets filled with soap, shampoo, and towels. He heard neighbors call out his name, but he kept running.

Hot tears pricked his eyes, and his legs burned. His head didn't know where to go, but his feet knew. They carried him to the place where he had always known peace—Grandfather's workshop.

Hiroshi stopped in the doorway, his chest heaving with every breath. He pressed his hands against either side of the doorframe.

Silence. He stepped inside, and the sweet smell of bamboo greeted him. Muted light from the eastern window illuminated the squares of *washi* paper that stood in a stack below the shelves of paint—red paint mostly, the lucky color of the dragon. Hiroshi's pounding heartbeat started to slow. He walked over to the box of bamboo poles and ran his hand along their cool, smooth surface.

How can we move to America? Everything is here.

15

He sank onto Grandfather's stool and gazed at the kites hanging from the ceiling. Colorful geometric designs and fierce ancient warriors stared back at him—designs that Grandfather had painted for his customers. The warriors' glares had always spooked Hiroshi. But today he read fear in their eyes—fear that they'd be left behind in Japan.

"Don't look at me," Hiroshi said to the kites. "I'm not the one who wants to go to America."

Hiroshi heard footsteps shuffling up the path. Only ancient Hakata-san shuffled—he must be coming for late morning tea with Grandfather. Hiroshi stood to greet the old man. But when the footsteps stopped, it was Grandfather's face that appeared in the doorway.

"Hiroshi?"

"Grandfather?" Hiroshi took a step forward, expecting to see Hakata-san over Grandfather's shoulder. But Grandfather was alone.

Hiroshi swallowed hard. "Did you know?"

Grandfather sighed. "They told you, then," he said softly as he stepped into the shop. "I knew about the job offer, yes."

Hiroshi focused on his bare feet to avoid Grandfather's gaze. *Grandfather knew all along and never said a word.* Anger seeped into Hiroshi's heart. He met Grandfather's eyes. "Then why were we at the hill this morning, practicing for the kite battle?"

Grandfather lifted his hands then let them drop. "I was sure your father would wait until after the battle. I was hoping . . ."

He had never seen Grandfather look so frail. Hiroshi's anger began fade. "But he's your son, Grandfather. He should listen to you."

The beginnings of a smile played on Grandfather's lips. "Your

16

father is a grown man, and he is doing what he thinks is right for his family. The right way is not always the easiest."

"You don't want to go, either, do you?"

Grandfather stood so still that Hiroshi thought maybe he hadn't heard the question. Then Grandfather said, "Let's take a walk, shall we?"

They followed the path in silence up to the practice hill where they had flown the dragon kite earlier that morning. Now that the kite fliers had returned home for lunch, the seagulls had the sky all to themselves. Hiroshi tried to memorize the slope of the hill—the way it rolled down to the village that touched Tachibana Bay. Boats bobbed as fishermen hauled their nets into waiting hulls. The sun glinted off silvery fish that flopped and squirmed in the bottom of the boats. Shouts of the fishmongers and the scent of salt water drifted up the hill with the wind. *How can we live anywhere but here?*

Grandfather and Hiroshi lay side by side on their usual spot in the grass and studied the sky.

"I guess it doesn't matter what the wind does today," Hiroshi said. "Or tomorrow."

"There is wind in America, you know."

But it would be different from Japanese wind, Hiroshi was sure.

"We will bring the dragon kite with us," Grandfather said.

"What about your workshop?"

"I can ship all of my things. We shall still make kites, Hiroshi. You will see."

"But it won't be the same." Grandfather didn't reply. "I won't know anyone there. I won't have any friends."

"Your uncle lives in Virginia."

17

Hiroshi's father had three brothers—Second Uncle lived in Tokyo, Third Uncle lived up north in Hokkaido, and then there was First Uncle—Father's twin. The brother whose name appeared on many of the *rokkaku* trophies in Grandfather's workshop. The one who had moved to America before Hiroshi was born. The one no one ever talked about.

Grandfather spoke, his eyes closed. "You will meet your American aunt and your cousin, Sorano, who is your age. They are already making plans to help us settle in." He opened his eyes and smiled at Hiroshi. "Sorano will be in your class at school. So you see? We will be with family."

Great. The only person I'll know at school will be a girl. Hiroshi turned his gaze back to the clouds. And then he saw it.

"Look!" Grandfather turned his head, following the line of Hiroshi's outstretched arm. "Do you see it?" Hiroshi whispered.

"I see it." Grandfather pointed. "There's the head, the body, and there . . . there's the tail trailing behind him."

"I've never seen a dragon-shaped cloud before."

"Neither have I, in all my years." They watched the dragon parade across the sky. "The dragon is a creature of the sea," Grandfather said. "When it takes to the sky, it is looking for something precious it has lost. When it finds what it was looking for, it returns to the sea in the form of rain."

"Do you think it's looking for us?"

"I don't think so, Hiroshi. If it were, we would feel it in our hearts."

"But maybe he knows you and I were both born in the year of the dragon. Maybe he knows we're—"

"Two of a kind." Grandfather smiled. "Maybe." They watched

18

the wind carry the dragon out to sea. "Hiroshi, there is something I must tell you."

Hiroshi didn't take his eyes off the cloud. "What is it?"

Grandfather sat up. "I am afraid it is my fault that we are moving to America."

Hiroshi sat up, too. "But I thought we were moving because of Father's job."

Grandfather nodded. "He did ask to be transferred to Washington, DC. His company has an American branch there."

Hiroshi frowned. "Then I don't understand. Why would Father ask to go to America?"

Grandfather plucked a blade of grass. He twirled it between his thumb and finger, then opened his hand to let the wind carry it across the hill. "I am not well, Hiroshi."

Hiroshi frowned. "But why do we have to go all the way to America? Can't you go to the doctor here?"

Grandfather picked another blade of grass. "The doctors here say they cannot help me. But we have spoken with some American doctors who have developed a new treatment. They say I am a good candidate."

A gust of wind slammed into Hiroshi, and he braced himself. "But . . . I mean, you'll be okay, won't you?"

Grandfather didn't speak as the gulls cried out. Then he turned to Hiroshi and said, "I am sure I will be fine." Grandfather smiled, but it wasn't a true smile.

The wind paused, leaving Hiroshi's unspoken questions hanging in the air.

5
Skye

Skye shivered as she stepped out of the warm car into the cold February drizzle.

"Don't forget this." Her mom handed Skye a water bottle through the open window. "We'll park and then see you out there."

Her dad leaned forward. "Good luck!"

Skye nodded her thanks, still barely awake, and wondered who was crazy enough to schedule a soccer game this early in the morning. At least these Sunday scrimmages didn't interfere with Japanese class. Why did the summer All-Star games have to be on Saturdays?

She trudged toward the field, pulling her sweatshirt hood up over her ponytail. Saturdays or Sundays—it didn't matter. She would pass those stupid exams and qualify for the afternoon Japanese class this summer. She had to.

"Hey, Skye! Wait up!" She turned to see Amber jogging toward her. It was too cold to stop moving altogether, so Skye shuffled backward until Amber caught up. "I love morning games," Amber said, stretching her arms above her head. *Of course you do,* Skye thought. Amber could afford to be perky—her All-Star spot didn't depend on passing any Japanese exams.

"Let's go, girls!" Coach Tess waved them over. "All right,

0

practice your passes in groups of three—five minutes, slow and easy," Coach Tess said. "Then I want four laps—straight jogging for the first lap, pick it up for the second, then dribble the ball around for the last two. Off you go!"

After the warm-up, Skye knew she'd pushed herself harder than usual. With every kick, she'd tried to imagine herself scoring a goal on the All-Star team. But visions of Japanese *kanji* characters swam in her head. At least now she wasn't cold, and she was ready to go. When the whistle blew, Skye blocked out anything and everything Japanese. She'd earned her spot on the summer All-Star team, and she would show her parents she couldn't let it go.

The first half sped by, and the score was tied—so were Skye and Amber, at two goals each. Now their team needed one more goal for the win. When the whistle blew for the second half, Skye heard her parents cheering. She frowned. If she lost her spot on the All-Star team this summer, it would be their fault. But seeing them huddled beneath their giant rainbow umbrella, grinning and yelling her name, she couldn't stay mad. She gave them a wave, then jogged onto the field and into position.

After almost thirty frustrating minutes of more drizzle and no goals, Skye finally saw her chance. The ball sailed toward her and she leaped, trapping it with her knee so it dropped right in front of her. Dribbling and weaving, Skye kept the goal in sight—twenty yards, fifteen, ten . . . With her focus on the goal, she almost missed seeing the defender bearing down on her from the left. Skye faked right, then skirted around the defender and took the shot. GOAL! The whistle blew, and Skye's teammates raced to her with grins and high fives.

She headed back toward the bench, where Coach Tess was

waiting. After their consolation cheer for the other team, both teams lined up midfield for high fives. Skye walked over to her parents on the sidelines.

"Congratulations!" Skye's mom said, pulling her into a hug.

Her dad smiled. "Skye! That was hands down the best game I've ever seen you play."

Skye grinned. "I felt great out there. Coach Tess says I'm totally ready for All-Stars this summer."

Her parents' smiles faded. "Honey," her mom started, then sighed.

Skye shook her head and flung her backpack over her shoulder. "Don't say it, Mom." She strode toward the car, leaving her parents behind.

Hiroshi spotted First Uncle right away. Most people waiting at the airport had smiles or balloons or bunches of flowers, calling and waving as loved ones came through the doors. Others held name signs, scanning the arriving passengers for any raised eyebrow of recognition.

First Uncle belonged to neither group—maybe that was why he stood out. He kept shifting from one foot to the other, crossing his arms one second, then putting his hands in his pockets the next.

Mother placed her hand on Hiroshi's shoulder. "There he is," she said, leaning down to whisper. "Your father's brother."

First Uncle hadn't spotted them yet, which gave Hiroshi more time to study him as they made their way across the scuffed floor. First Uncle and Father were fraternal twins, so Hiroshi knew they wouldn't look exactly alike. But how could two brothers look so different? Father was tall and lanky. First Uncle was at least a hand shorter, and stocky.

Hiroshi slowed. What should he say to First Uncle? What would First Uncle say to him?

But when First Uncle spotted them, he didn't seem to notice Hiroshi at all. He was looking at Grandfather, like he was trying to figure out who he was. Maybe after twelve years, he'd forgotten what Grandfather looked like.

Father greeted First Uncle with a bow. "Brother. You are looking well." He sounded formal, like he was talking to one of Hiroshi's teachers.

"As are you, Brother." First Uncle matched Father's bow. "*Irrasshai.* Welcome to America."

They sure weren't acting like brothers—more like strangers. Nothing like the easy, friendly way Father acted around his other brothers.

First Uncle's nervous smile melted into a real one as he greeted Mother. Whatever family argument there'd been all those years ago must not have involved her.

First Uncle's smile faded as he turned to Grandfather. First Uncle bowed deeply, holding the bow until Grandfather touched his shoulder. When First Uncle straightened, he looked sad. Sad—and sorry for something. But what?

The sounds of the crowd seemed to pause as Hiroshi waited for Grandfather to speak. Grandfather opened his mouth, closed it again, and breathed in. And then he spoke: "I have allowed a misunderstanding to come between us. It is time we let it go."

With those words, First Uncle's real smile returned.

The airport sounds came flooding back, and Hiroshi shared his own real smile with Father.

"You must be Hiroshi, of course." First Uncle started to bow, and Hiroshi rushed to complete his bow first.

"It is an honor to meet you, First Uncle." First Uncle laughed, and Hiroshi couldn't help thinking how American he looked—that laugh exposed all his teeth, clear back to the molars.

"You look exactly like your father did at your age, Hiro-chan. And you sound just like him, too." Hiroshi didn't know if that was supposed to be a compliment or not, but he thanked First Uncle, just in case.

"Are we all ready?" First Uncle asked. "Cathy and Sorano are looking forward to meeting you."

Cathy? Trying to pronounce that one would take some practice. Luckily Hiroshi could just call her *Aunt*. He had practiced saying it in English and hoped she would be pleased. At least Sorano had a Japanese name.

Leaving the airport, the first thing Hiroshi noticed was the sky—scattered shreds of soggy, gray winter clouds mixed with patches of blue. Hiroshi trailed his suitcase behind him, wheeling it over the curb. The wind gusted, giving Hiroshi a push, and then scurried away. It was as if this American wind were introducing itself, showing off its strength.

"Good kite-flying wind, Hiroshi." Grandfather placed his hand on Hiroshi's shoulder. Father, Mother, and First Uncle walked ahead, lost in conversation.

Hiroshi nodded. "I guess." He thought of the box wrapped in brown paper he and Grandfather had packed with care back in Japan. Inside that box, the dragon kite slumbered. *Where is the box now? Has it already arrived in America, ahead of us? What will happen when the dragon wakes? Will it know its way around an American sky?*

They arrived at First Uncle's car. No—it was bigger than a car. It was more like a van, but wider and longer than minivans in Japan. Hiroshi figured First Uncle must have a lot of money—not only to have a car this size, but also to afford a place to park it.

Hiroshi helped Father and First Uncle with the suitcases. Grandfather went to lift a suitcase into the back, but Mother rested her hand on his arm.

"It has been a long trip. You will do me a favor if you wait here with me." Mother always knew how to turn things around so that helping Grandfather made it seem like he was really helping her.

First Uncle held open the driver's door for Grandfather. "Father, please. This seat is for you."

Grandfather frowned and crossed his hands in an X, tapping one hand against the other twice. "It would be best if you would drive, Issei."

First Uncle looked confused for a moment, then laughed. "Father, this is the passenger side."

Hiroshi peered in the window and saw that the steering wheel was on the wrong side of the car. But First Uncle's car was a Ford—an American car, so it made sense. A glance at the other cars in the parking lot told Hiroshi that the other cars were all the same—even the Japanese cars had the steering wheel on the left.

As First Uncle pulled out of the parking lot, Grandfather turned to Hiroshi and raised his arms. "Look—no hands!" Hiroshi laughed; it *did* seem like Grandfather was in the driver's seat without a steering wheel.

First Uncle pulled through a booth and handed a ticket to a lady sitting behind a window. She said something to First Uncle, and a sign in the window flashed $4.50. Was that a lot of money? Four and a half yen was close to nothing, but he knew American dollars were different. First Uncle said something in English to the lady, and they pulled away.

Grandfather looked at First Uncle with a mixture of pride and

26

confusion. "So that is English?" First Uncle nodded, keeping his eyes on the road. "Then you are a good English speaker," Grandfather said, like this was an undisputable fact.

First Uncle laughed. "I still make mistakes, after all these years."

Mother nudged Hiroshi. "You will learn English just like First Uncle. You will study hard." The hum of the motor was enough to lull Hiroshi to sleep, and he fought to keep his eyes open. Learning English was the last thing he wanted to think about.

"How far away are the monuments? And the White House?" Grandfather asked, looking out the window.

"We are actually far from the city, Father—about thirty miles."

Hiroshi tried to remember how to convert miles to kilometers, but the numbers were jumbled in his head. "So why is the airport called Dulles? Is that a town?"

Grandfather looked back and nodded—he must have thought it was a good question, too.

First Uncle looked perplexed. "You know, Hiro-chan, I'm not sure. I think it may be named after someone, but I'm not sure who." Hiroshi didn't dare look at his parents. He had just asked a question that First Uncle didn't know the answer to. Hiroshi hadn't meant to be disrespectful. But First Uncle laughed. "We'll have to Google that one when we get home."

Google? Apparently, America did have some Japanese things.

Hiroshi must have nodded off, because Father had to nudge him awake as they pulled into First Uncle's neighborhood. Hiroshi blinked. How long had he been asleep? He looked at the houses parading outside his window. They looked just like the American houses in the movies, three or four styles that repeated like a pattern. Each was surrounded by its own park—grass, flowers, bushes, and trees.

The adults had all fallen quiet. Hiroshi was sure Grandfather and his parents were as tired as he was. First Uncle looked like he was concentrating. On what, Hiroshi wasn't sure.

They pulled into the driveway of a brick house. The park in front looked even fancier than the other houses' parks—a stone path led to the front door, and bushes no higher than Hiroshi's ankles lined the path. It was too early for flowers, but Hiroshi recognized the cherry tree that would bloom in the next month or two. In fact, every plant looked as if it had come from the garden outside Grandfather's workshop in Japan.

When Grandfather got out of the car, he stopped and stared. Hiroshi stood next to him, remembering their garden and wondering who would water it when the spring sun came. Grandfather's eyes seemed full of remembering, too.

The front door swung open, and the spell was broken. A woman wearing a nervous smile stepped out. She looked like she didn't know what to do with her hands—folding her hands one second, brushing her straw-colored hair back the next. She finally bent somewhere between a nod and a bow, like she couldn't decide which one to do.

"Hello. *Irrasshaimase.*"

The Japanese word for "welcome" sounded out of place coming from this American face. First Uncle skipped up the step and stood next to her.

Grandfather bowed and said that it was nice to meet Aunt Cathy. Hiroshi wondered if she'd understood him, but she bowed anyway and said she was happy to meet him, too, in careful Japanese.

28

"Hello." Father stepped forward, bowed, then held out his hand. "It is a pleasure to meet you, Mrs. Tsuki." It was strange to hear English come from Father's lips and see him shake hands like an American.

Aunt Cathy seemed relieved. She shook Father's hand like she didn't want to let go. "Please, call me Cathy."

Mother was next. She had been practicing English for the last month and looked like she was about to take an exam. She made it through, "It is nice to meet you." Then she looked back at Hiroshi, beckoning him to the front.

Hiroshi knew Americans didn't bow, so he offered his hand, as Father had done. "It is nice to meet you, Aunt."

Aunt Cathy smiled and said in rehearsed-sounding Japanese: "Please. It would be an honor if you would call me *Oba-chan*."

Hiroshi was surprised that she preferred the Japanese word for aunt, but he smiled back. "Yes, *Oba-chan*. Okay."

She led them into the house and said something about Sorano, her daughter. First Uncle translated: "Sorano will be down in a moment. She arrived from soccer practice not long ago, and she is upstairs changing."

Hiroshi helped First Uncle and Father with the suitcases, which they left at the bottom of the stairs.

"Come," First Uncle said. "Please have something to eat, and then I will show you to your rooms. You must be tired." Hiroshi wasn't even sure what time it was supposed to be. It had to be afternoon, but he felt like he could lie down and sleep all the way through to the next day.

As Aunt Cathy headed toward the kitchen, Mother whispered, "Hiroshi, go and get the gifts from my red carry-on bag. They are in the main compartment." Hiroshi headed back to the pile of luggage near the stairs. He rummaged around in Mother's bag, found the gifts, then stood. He turned and crashed right into something hard. The gifts went flying, and Hiroshi staggered back, falling onto a suitcase. When he recovered, a girl stood over him, face red, hand extended.

"Sorry," she said. "Are you okay?"

So this was his American cousin.

How was Skye supposed to know that Hiroshi would whirl around just as she was jumping down the last step to say hello?

"*Gomen nasai,*" she managed, thankful she had remembered how to say "I'm sorry" in Japanese. She offered her hand to help him up, but he scrambled to his feet on his own. They bent to retrieve the scattered gifts at the same time and almost bumped heads.

"*Gomen nasai,*" they said in unison.

Skye laughed. She couldn't help it. Luckily, Hiroshi laughed, too.

"You are Sorano?"

So he speaks English! Now she wouldn't have to worry about coming up with the right words in Japanese.

"Yes, my name is Sorano, but all my friends call me Skye. I mean, you're my cousin, so I guess you can call me Sorano. But I like Skye better."

Hiroshi stared at her, eyebrows raised.

Uh-oh. Calling herself Skye had probably confused him. Or maybe she'd been talking too fast.

"Sorano?" He looked unsure.

Skye shrugged. "Either one. Sorano, Skye." He nodded, but she could tell he was still confused. "Um, Sorano is fine." They gathered the gifts, and Skye shook a few, praying she wouldn't hear the rattle of broken glass. So far, so good. "I'll help you carry these, okay?"

He held out his free hand. "*Arigato gozaimasu.* I can take them in," he continued in Japanese. "I think my mother wants to present them to you and your parents."

"Oh! Of course." Skye handed over the gifts.

When they entered the kitchen, the adults stopped talking and turned. Her dad came forward and put his arm around her. "I see you've met your cousin." He spoke in Japanese.

Skye nodded. "*Hai.*" Her dad waited, like she was supposed to say more than just "yes." Her aunt, uncle, and grandfather waited, smiling, like they expected her to break into song—maybe the Japanese national anthem, whatever that was.

Her dad spoke to her in English out of the side of his mouth: "Don't forget what we practiced."

How could she forget? She'd memorized all the right things to say, and she'd even practiced bowing. Hands at her sides. Bend at the waist. Bow lower than the adults. Bow lowest for the grandfather. Good grief, it'd been like living in bowing boot camp for the last month.

With a nudge from her dad, she stepped forward. "I am Sk— Sorano." Now the relatives looked confused—probably thought her name was *Sksorano*. Better start again. "I am Sorano. Welcome to our home. It is a pleasure to meet you."

Now for the bow—but should she do a general bow, or bow to each person one at a time? She glanced at her dad for some kind of sign, but he obviously wasn't picking up her distress signal. Luckily Hiroshi's parents stepped forward and were still smiling, so that

32

had to be good. Although her dad had said that Japanese people always smile in public, even if they're sad or embarrassed.

"Sorano, it is a pleasure to finally meet you," Hiroshi's mother said with a smile. She had spoken slowly, like she was afraid Skye wouldn't understand her Japanese. When her aunt bowed, Skye bowed back. But how was she supposed to know right in the middle of bowing if her bow was lower than her aunt's? Skye ended up bowing with her head raised. Then she repeated the same thing all over again with Hiroshi's father.

When Skye glanced at Hiroshi, he had a grin on his face, but it didn't seem like a happy grin. Or an impressed grin at how well his American cousin was doing with his parents. No, Skye decided he was amused. There was probably a no-peeking-when-bowing rule.

Next came the grandfather. He looked younger than she'd imagined. Sure, he was wrinkly, and his hair was as white as milk. Only his eyebrows had traces of the black his hair must have been. But he didn't stoop, like lots of old people do, and he was tall, like Hiroshi's dad. His eyes were the youngest thing about him—bright and smiling. She was so busy studying his face that she forgot to bow at first. And she'd completely forgotten that she wasn't supposed to stare an adult right in the face.

"You are just as lovely as your mother, and your grandmother before you."

Lovely? No one had ever described her that way, except maybe her parents after they made her dress up for something. She wasn't pretty like the Ambers of the world, or even pretty like the Chinese American Lucy Lius of the world. Skye was somewhere in the middle—not Asian, not white. Caucasian applied perfectly to her—"Asian" hiding in a word meaning "white."

33

"*Arigato goziamasu,*" Skye said, thanking him for the compliment. "It is an honor to meet you." Now she remembered to bow, and this time she didn't look up. She had to hope that her bow was lower than her grandfather's.

"Please, come and have something to eat." Skye's dad pointed them toward the table.

They all murmured about how good the food looked and smelled. It should, since her mom had picked it up from Takahashi's Take-Out over on Little River Avenue. They always had the best Japanese food. Not that Skye liked most Japanese food, but she spied miso soup on the table, her favorite. At least she could use a spoon with the soup—she'd always been a little shaky when it came to chopsticks, like her mom.

"Why don't you sit next to Hiroshi?" her mom said.

"Excellent idea," her dad added in Japanese. "I'm sure Hiroshi will have many questions about school."

Skye only hoped she could answer his questions in Japanese without sounding like an idiot. Maybe he knew enough English so she wouldn't have to resort to Japanese. Although she was supposed to be practicing so she could pass the stupid exams.

As the plates were passed around, she tried to think of the Japanese words she'd need to answer Hiroshi's questions about school. She decided to start with the basics. "We'll be in the same class," she told him.

"For which subject?" He added some soba noodles into his bowl.

"All of them." Hiroshi looked surprised, so Skye tried to explain. "We have a different teacher for music, art—" *What did they call P.E.*

in Japan?—"and sports." Hiroshi nodded. "Oh, and computers." Luckily *computer* was the same word in Japanese.

Hiroshi set his chopsticks down. "You have the same teacher for everything else?"

Skye nodded. "Mrs. Garcia. She's nice. She knows you're coming, and she told me you'll have another teacher for English."

"Mrs. Garcia doesn't teach English?"

"Sure, she does. Kind of." This was turning out to be more complicated than Skye had thought. "It's more like she teaches everything *in* English—reading, writing, math, science, history." Skye picked up her spoon. "But you'll go to another teacher for help with the basics in English."

Speaking of basics, Skye decided that this conversation was exhausting. She couldn't remember the last time she'd uttered such a long string of words in Japanese.

Hiroshi looked disappointed. He switched to English: "I speak little English. I learn in school."

Skye hadn't meant to insult him when she said he needed the basics. Even though he did. Big time. "I'm still working on Japanese," Skye said. "I go to classes on Saturdays. I still make lots of mistakes."

When Hiroshi didn't argue with that, Skye wondered how many mistakes she'd already made in the last five minutes. She figured now would be a good time to stop talking and eat the soup.

Hiroshi seemed lost in his thoughts throughout the rest of the meal, and Skye was relieved she didn't have to come up with any more Japanese words.

Finally her dad said, "Cathy and Sorano have prepared the

35

rooms upstairs for you. I'll help you get settled in." Skye's aunt, uncle, and grandfather thanked Skye's mom for the meal. If only they knew they should have been thanking Mr. Takahashi and his Take-Out.

As they filed out of the kitchen, Skye stayed back to help her mom clear the table. Once she was sure the others were out of earshot, she whispered, "What are you going to do for lunch and dinner tomorrow? And the next day?"

Her mom sighed, and Skye realized how tiring the whole meal conversation must have been for her, too. "Good question. We can still order out a few more times, I suppose. The house they're renting over on Kemp Lane is ready for them to move in. But I'm sure they'll want a few days to get over jet lag before they get settled."

Skye pushed the takeout boxes further down into the trash. "I could help you smuggle the food into the house."

Her mom laughed and pulled Skye into a hug, kissing the top of her head. "I was so proud of you today. And I'm sure Hiroshi appreciated the effort you made to talk with him."

"He seems nice. I'm sure my Japanese will get better just by talking with him. And maybe it'll get so good that I won't have to take that morning class, so the All-Star schedule won't even be a problem."

Skye's mom loaded the dishwasher in silence, plate after plate, glass after glass.

"Mom, did you hear what I said?"

Her mom turned, dried her hands, and leaned against the counter. "Yes, talking with your relatives in Japanese will help, honey. But I just don't think it'll be enough." She walked over to the calendar and lifted the page. "You've only got a little over six weeks to get ready for the placement exams."

Skye didn't need to look at the calendar to know she had exactly forty-three days left.

She looked outside. The sky was still light. A perfect time to practice some backyard goals. Instead she went into the computer room, pulled out the hated list of the next hundred *kanji* she was supposed to memorize, and flopped into the chair. This was going to take a while.

寛 ○

Hiroshi awoke as soon as he hit the floor.

Where am I?

He squeezed his eyes shut, shook his head, then opened his eyes again. Instead of his futon, he saw sheets and blankets tangled at the foot of a high wooden bed. A photograph of Grandfather and Hiroshi holding a trophy was propped on the nightstand—the picture from last year's *rokkaku* battle. He felt the scratchy carpet underneath him instead of cool tatami mats that smelled of sweet grass. Of course—he was on the floor of his new American bedroom.

He heard a soft knock on his door.

"Come in."

Mother peered into the room. "Hiroshi, are you all right?" she asked, her brow furrowed.

He climbed back onto the bed and rubbed his shoulder. "I'm fine. I miss my futon." After a week in America, he still wasn't used to sleeping on such a high bed.

"There's not enough room in the closet to store a futon during the day." Mother came and sat next to him. "Things are different here, but we'll get used to it. It takes time." Hiroshi stared at the carpet. "Now that you're starting school, you'll make friends. And Sorano will be there to help."

School. The familiar knot clenched his gut again. "I don't know enough English. How can I make friends if I can't even talk to anyone?"

"You can practice what you learned in your English classes back home. Soon enough you'll have too many friends to count."

"I guess." Hiroshi thought about his classmates in Japan. They'd be starting sixth grade when the academic year began in April. Not Hiroshi. He was stuck in fifth grade again for another four months.

"Are you hungry? I've made your favorite breakfast." Even the thought of fish and rice didn't cheer him up. Mother smiled and rose from the bed. "I'll see you downstairs."

Hiroshi opened his closet door. He never thought he'd miss his school uniform, but at least getting dressed for school had always been easy. What did American kids wear to school? He should have asked Sorano. He chose a pair of jeans; Americans on television always wore jeans. And a red polo shirt—red would bring him luck. He took a deep breath, exhaled, and followed the scent of fish downstairs for breakfast.

Hiroshi stood in front of his new class, head down and cheeks burning. Mrs. Garcia spoke to the other fifth graders. Hiroshi didn't understand a thing she said. He wondered what Miss Dillon, his English teacher in Japan, would think. Mrs. Garcia smiled and pointed to him with an open hand. The only word he understood came out as "huh-RO-shee," with that hard American *r* sound.

He jumped when the class chorused, "Hello!" but at least he knew this word, too. He automatically bowed to his classmates. A few snickers broke the silence.

That's right—no bowing. Next time he would remember.

Mrs. Garcia spoke again to the students, frowning this time. They leaned over their desks and began writing in their notebooks. Hiroshi followed Mrs. Garcia to his desk, and he slid into his seat. She put her hand on Sorano's shoulder, who sat across the aisle from him. Mrs. Garcia said something to her, patted her shoulder, and walked away.

At least Hiroshi knew someone in this school. It didn't even matter that she was a girl and his cousin. In the days since he'd arrived in America, he'd asked Sorano every question he could think of about school. But now that he was here, he had questions he hadn't known to ask before. Why didn't the students wear uniforms? Why didn't they start the day with a class meeting? Why was everyone wearing their outdoor shoes inside? And the English class he was supposed to go to—when would that happen? Maybe Sorano wouldn't mind asking the teacher for him.

He leaned across the aisle and whispered her name. When she turned, he asked about his English class. A boy with spiky yellow hair sitting in front of Sorano turned around. He looked with wide eyes from Sorano to Hiroshi.

Sorano glared at the spiky-haired boy, then hissed something at him. He smirked and started whispering to the girl sitting in front of him. Hiroshi couldn't help but feel like he had done something wrong. The boy seemed to be making fun of Sorano, but Hiroshi couldn't figure out why. Or was the boy making fun of him?

Sorano stood up. She passed by Hiroshi's desk and whispered in Japanese, "Maybe you should call me Skye here at school." Then she headed off toward the pencil sharpener. Hiroshi sat staring at the stack of school supplies on his desk. How was he supposed to remember to call Sorano by a different name? Had the spiky-haired boy been laughing at her name?

Sorano—Skye—slipped back into her seat just as the classroom television came on. Two students appeared on the screen. It looked like they were announcing the news, except they didn't bow first. They held up a weather forecast sign, with the high temperature of forty-five degrees. That seemed really hot, but Hiroshi knew that Fahrenheit was different from Celsius. When a picture of the American flag appeared on the screen, everyone stood, put their hand on their chest, and started reciting something in a monotone. Hiroshi had no idea what they were saying. When it was over, Hiroshi was the only one left standing. He quickly sat back down, hoping no one had noticed.

Mrs. Garcia began the math lesson. Hiroshi had always hated math. Not that it was difficult—just boring. There was always only one right answer. Not like art. In art there were a million ways to do things. Hiroshi remembered watching Grandfather paint kites for customers. He'd painted whatever they asked for, but he always added a personal touch, too. Like the time when Yamamoto-san asked for a carp, and Grandfather had painted the scales in a rainbow of colors. No one ever minded when Grandfather did his own thing, because his own thing was what made the kites so special.

41

Hiroshi almost jumped when he realized Mrs. Garcia was standing next to his desk, handing him a worksheet covered with numbers. At least he knew what to do—he didn't need English to do equations.

"Thank you, Teacher," he said. The English words felt strange on his tongue.

Mrs. Garcia smiled but shook her head. She patted her chest with her hand. "MI-sses Gar-SEE-uh." Hiroshi nodded. He already knew her name; what was she doing?

Another student raised his hand. "Mrs. Garcia?"

"Yes?" She smiled and headed over to the boy's desk. She didn't seem to mind being called by her name. Hiroshi couldn't imagine calling her Mrs. Garcia; it was disrespectful—too familiar. Besides, how was he supposed to pronounce a name with an American *r* in it?

He started to write his name in *kanji* characters on the work-sheet, then erased it and wrote it in English. He had almost worked his way to the bottom of the page when another teacher entered the room. Mrs. Garcia waved the teacher over to her desk, where they spoke in low voices.

"Skye? Hiroshi?" Mrs. Garcia beckoned.

Hiroshi glanced at Sor—Skye. She stood and motioned for him to follow. When they reached the front of the room, Mrs. Garcia said something to Skye, who then whispered to Hiroshi in Japanese: "This is your ESL teacher—English as a second language. His name's Mr. Jacobs."

Skye folded her arms and took a step back. The class had fallen silent. Mr. Jacobs spoke to Skye, then she translated in a voice even softer than before. "You have ESL class every morning from nine to ten thirty. Then you come back here for the rest of the day." She looked from Mrs. Garcia back to Mr. Jacobs, as if to ask if that would be all.

"Thank you," Mrs. Garcia said. Skye hurried back to her seat, leaving Hiroshi standing there.

Hiroshi knew she was embarrassed. Was it her mistakes in Japanese? He didn't care about that. He knew he was about to make even more mistakes in English.

"Hello, Hiroshi." Mr. Jacobs grinned and offered Hiroshi his hand. He decided Mr. Jacobs looked too young to be a teacher.

"Hello, Teacher." Hiroshi bowed, then remembered to shake Mr. Jacobs's hand.

"Come with me." Mr. Jacobs grinned and headed for the door.

Hiroshi hoped the other ESL students wouldn't be too far ahead of him in English. What if he couldn't keep up? Outside the classroom five other students waited in the hallway. As they followed Mr. Jacobs down the hall, some whispered to each other in English, and others in a language that sounded like Spanish. Were they whispering about him?

Mr. Jacobs strode into the ESL room. "Let's take our seats, everyone."

Hiroshi noticed the artwork right away—drawings, paintings, collages. They filled one wall from ceiling to floor. Hiroshi smiled. Another wall had a chalkboard surrounded by groups of index cards with English words and pictures.

The students sat at a U-shaped table, and Hiroshi took the last empty place at the end. Mr. Jacobs gave him a notebook and a marker, then pointed to a blank box on the cover.

"Name." He smiled. "Your name goes here." As soon as Hiroshi printed his name on the front, Mr. Jacobs introduced him to the group. The other students took turns saying their strange names—not one was Japanese. He'd never remember them all.

Mr. Jacobs gave every student five cards, each with a picture. Hiroshi looked at his cards: a shirt, a jacket, a pair of shoes, a hat, and a scarf. *Is this some kind of joke? This is baby work.* But Mr. Jacobs wasn't laughing. He began writing a list of clothing items on the board—all words Hiroshi recognized from Miss Dillon's English classes way back in first grade.

Hiroshi watched as the boy next to him wrote his name: Ravi. The boy copied down the English words. Hiroshi sighed and picked up his pencil. At least his classmates in Japan couldn't see him now.

Mr. Jacobs clapped once and said something to the girl sitting closest to the board. The girl nodded and smiled, then held up a card with a picture of a pair of blue trousers. She said, "I am wearing blue pants."

Hiroshi's eyes widened. How embarrassing for the girl; she had just told the teacher she was wearing underwear. What would Mr. Jacobs say?

"Good, Maria." Mr. Jacobs nodded.

What? Hiroshi stifled a giggle. Miss Dillon had taught them that *pants* meant underwear. But Miss Dillon was English, not American, and she had said Americans sometimes have different ways of saying things. Hiroshi looked at his cards again. At least he didn't have a picture of trousers.

When Maria finished with her cards, Mr. Jacobs went on to the next student. A wave of panic rolled through Hiroshi. Four more students, and then it would be his turn. Hiroshi knew the words to say, but what if his pronunciation was off? The other students'

44

English sounded perfect. He studied his cards again. His hands began to tremble, so he spread his cards on the table and stuck his hands under his legs. He recited his lines over and over in his head until Mr. Jacobs said, "Hiroshi, what are you wearing?"

Hiroshi swallowed. He pointed to the card with the picture of a shirt and said, "I wear a shirt."

"Excellent, Hiroshi. What color is your shirt?"

Hiroshi relaxed his shoulders. The teacher was pleased with his answer! "Red. My shirt is red."

Mr. Jacobs nodded. "What else are you wearing?"

Hiroshi went through the other cards until he got to the last one. He pointed to the card with shoes. "I am wearing shoe."

Mr. Jacobs peeked under the table. "And what color are your shoes, Hiroshi?"

Shoes. He should have said *shoes,* not *shoe.* How could he have been so stupid? He stared at the card. "My shoes are brown." He made sure to say *shoes* a bit louder than the other words, hoping Mr. Jacobs would hear that he had corrected himself.

Mr. Jacobs held out his hand in front of Hiroshi, palm up. Keeping his chin down, Hiroshi raised his eyes and saw Mr. Jacobs' wide smile. Hiroshi lifted his head. He didn't know what to do. Was he supposed to give the teacher something?

"Give me five, Hiroshi. Nice job with *shoes!*" Hiroshi knew what this meant from watching American movies. But giving five to a *teacher?* He snuck a glance at the other students, who were all grinning. Hiroshi raised his hand, then hesitated.

"Go on," said Mr. Jacobs. "Don't leave me hanging!" He chuckled. Hiroshi slapped his hand down on Mr. Jacob's palm. He tried to imagine what his fifth-grade teacher from last year would say—

45

serious Motomashi Sensei with a face like a raisin. He bit the inside of his cheek to cut off the laughter that threatened to escape; he didn't want Mr. Jacobs to think he was laughing at him.

But a moment later Hiroshi's urge to laugh fizzled when Mr. Jacobs handed out books. He said something to the class, and Hiroshi recognized the word "homework." He stared at the cover—a picture of a boy pulling on his socks under the title *Tim Gets Dressed.* There couldn't be more than ten pages in the whole story. Hiroshi opened the cover and scanned the first page: "Tim puts on a shirt." Now the second page: "Tim puts on his socks." It wasn't even a real story; it was a book for first graders, not fifth graders. He slid it into his notebook. Speaking English was difficult, but reading in English was easy. When he could speak more English, he would ask Mr. Jacobs for a harder book. One with chapters and no pictures.

Next Mr. Jacobs handed out blank sheets of paper and colored pencils. He explained something to the group, but Hiroshi didn't understand. The other students began sketching. Hiroshi snuck a sideways glance at Ravi, who was bent over his paper drawing two careful circles. When Ravi lifted his head, Hiroshi's eyes darted back to his own paper; he didn't want Ravi to think he was trying to copy him.

But Ravi leaned over. "I draw a car," he whispered. Ravi moved his pencil across the paper, and the outline of a race car appeared. Was the assignment to a draw a car? Which kind of car? Any car?

Hiroshi was about to sneak a look at another student's paper when Mr. Jacobs pulled up a chair and sat across from him with a sheet of paper. Mr. Jacobs drew a basketball and hoop, then held up the paper. "I like basketball." Then he tapped Hiroshi's blank paper. "What do you like, Hiroshi?"

Hiroshi nodded; he knew exactly what he would draw. He picked up three pencils—different shades of green—and began with the grassy hill. Then he sketched himself, Grandfather, and finally the dragon kite.

"This is you." Mr. Jacobs tapped the figure of Hiroshi in the picture. He slid his finger over to Grandfather. "Who is this?"

Hiroshi nodded. "My grandfather."

Mr. Jacobs pointed to the grassy hill. "Where is this place?"

Hiroshi's throat tightened. "My village. In Japan."

"You like kites?"

Hiroshi looked at the drawing. "Yes." He nodded. He thought of the exact words he wanted to say, so he wouldn't make a mistake: "I like kites."

But he wanted to say so much more. He wanted to tell Mr. Jacobs about the kite battle he had to miss because he'd moved to America. He wanted to explain that the dragon kite was the first one he had made himself. Well, mostly himself—Grandfather had helped a little. He wanted to say that Grandfather was a *rokkaku* champion and Hiroshi's best friend. And that he hoped Grandfather would get better soon so they could keep flying kites together.

"Yes," Hiroshi repeated. "I like kites."

What a jerk. Kevin Donovan had never been Skye's favorite person, but she'd always felt kind of sorry for him. He didn't really have any friends, and now Skye could see why. Ever since she had translated something for Hiroshi that morning, Kevin wouldn't leave her alone. "Ching chang wong wang!" He snickered, obviously pleased with himself.

"That doesn't even mean anything." Skye rolled her eyes, hoping no one else had heard him. As luck would have it, she had to peer around his big head to copy the reading homework from the board. But whenever she tried to look, he blocked her way.

Skye sighed. "Cut it out. I can't see the board."

"Why don't you ask your Chinese boyfriend what it says when he gets back from ESL class?"

"He's not my boyfriend; he's my cousin. And he's not Chinese, duh. He's Japanese."

"Whatever."

Ignore him. Ignore him. Ignore him.

Mrs. Garcia clapped once. "Class, clear your desks for the science quiz." Skye moaned along with the others. But at least Kevin wouldn't be allowed to speak during the quiz—that was a bonus.

Kevin turned around again. "So are you Japanese, or what?"

Honestly. Doesn't he ever take a bullying break?

"Why don't you just leave her alone, Kevin?" Amber sat two seats in front of Kevin. If she'd heard the whole conversation, Skye wondered who else had been listening. Skye shot her a grateful smile, and Amber grinned back. "If you must know, Skye is Japanese. She was probably speaking Japanese to the new kid." Amber turned back around.

Skye probably should have been grateful that Amber had defended her. But she'd called Skye "Japanese." Okay, so Skye's dad was Japanese, and she spoke the language—kind of. But that didn't make *her* Japanese. She'd never even been to Japan.

Mrs. Garcia walked down the rows, handing out science quizzes. Diagrams of plant and animal cells—gross. They all looked like Kevin Donovan's head.

Five minutes into the quiz, Hiroshi and the other ESL kids came back into the room.

"Skye?" Mrs. Garcia called. She waved Skye to the front of the room. Skye sighed. She'd have to translate. Again. She turned her quiz over and stood up. The ESL kids headed straight to the computers, except for Hiroshi, who looked lost.

As Skye approached Kevin's desk, he had his chin in his hand, like he was concentrating on his quiz. But when she walked by, he sneered at her.

Ignore him.

When Skye and Hiroshi met at the teacher's desk, Mrs. Garcia smiled. "Skye, I am so glad that you can translate for Hiroshi throughout the day. I'm sure he's relieved to have help from his own cousin."

Not again. Skye concentrated on Mrs. Garcia's shoes—red and

49

shiny with a short heel. She tried to imagine Kevin wearing them, instead. She almost grinned.

"Would you please tell Hiroshi he'll be going to the computer station right after ESL each day? I'd like you to help him navigate his way around the Kid Science site. Go ahead and show him the interactive cell page we did last week."

Skye leaned in closer to Hiroshi, wishing Kevin wasn't witnessing this whole exchange, yet knowing he was. She translated the best she could, then risked a glance over her shoulder. Sure enough, half the class was staring, including Kevin. And even Amber.

Come on, people! The show's over. Back to cell parts! But vacuoles and cell membranes apparently weren't as much fun as gawking at the new kid or listening to Skye stumble her way through another language.

"It should only take a few minutes to show him how to log on, and then you'll have plenty of time to finish your quiz," Mrs. Garcia said. Skye nodded, feeling the flush of red to the roots of her hair. "Oh, and would you please tell Hiroshi that if he has any questions at any time, he should feel free to ask you?" Skye didn't have to glance over her shoulder this time to know the whole class was staring at her back. No pencil scratching. No eraser rubbing. Silence.

She leaned in closer to Hiroshi, then remembered Kevin's idiotic comment about Hiroshi being her boyfriend. Taking a tiny step back, she translated Mrs. Garcia's words, keeping her voice as quiet as she could. She knew she was making mistakes, but she just wanted to get this over with.

Hiroshi nodded.

"Thank you, Skye," Mrs. Garcia said, finally ending the translation torture.

Skye led Hiroshi to the computer station, which was, thankfully, about as far away from Kevin as possible. She showed Hiroshi how to get to the Kid Science site, then walked back to her desk, eyes down.

She knew it had to be hard for Hiroshi—being the new kid and not speaking English. *But it's no picnic for me, either.*

Hiroshi smelled the cafeteria before he saw it. Walking in line with his class, he caught the odor of some kind of meat mingled with lemony-scented floor cleaner. Voices bounced from one wall to the other, up to the high ceiling, and back down again.

This was nothing like lunchtime in his classroom last year.

As his class filed by the tables, Hiroshi didn't see any place mats—the other kids just set their trays right on the tables. The line snaked into the kitchen area, where several kinds of food sat behind a Plexiglas barrier. Ladies in uniforms did the serving—not classmates in white aprons, masks, and hats.

As he waited in line, Hiroshi dug his hand into his pocket and came up with his lunch money. He stared at the American coins and tried to remember how much each was worth. The only numerals on them were years. That was no help. He knew the quarter was worth the most because it was the biggest. The second biggest had to be worth ten cents. The next smallest must be five cents, and then there was the one-cent penny.

"Hello? You're next."

Hiroshi felt a poke in his back. He turned and saw a red-haired boy standing there.

"Take one. You're up."

52

Hiroshi looked past the boy to where Skye stood. She nodded toward the trays, then went back to talking to the girl next to her.

When Hiroshi didn't move, the boy rolled his eyes. He picked up a pink Styrofoam tray and handed it to Hiroshi. "Here—you need these, too." He put a napkin and a plastic fork and spoon on Hiroshi's tray.

Hiroshi nodded. "Thank you." He listened as the boy spoke to the cafeteria lady and pointed to the spaghetti. She wiped her brow with the back of her hand, then dug a huge spoon that looked like an ice cream scoop into the mass of wet noodles. She dumped the spaghetti into a Styrofoam bowl.

"Sauce?" The lady sounded bored.

The boy shrugged. "Yeah." She plunged a ladle into a pot splattered with red sauce, poured some onto the mound of noodles with a practiced turn of her wrist, and plopped the bowl onto the counter. The boy set the bowl on his tray, then slid it farther down the line.

"Next?" The lady tucked a stray tuft of fuzzy gray hair into her hairnet.

Hiroshi looked from the pan of spaghetti to another that held some kind of meat. At least he thought it might be meat—it was hard to tell with all that lumpy brown sauce. He pointed. "Please spaghetti." The lady repeated her ritual, and Hiroshi moved down the line.

"Bread?" Another lady offered a roll with a pair of tongs.

Hiroshi's stomach rumbled. "Thank you." Next he chose a small plastic bowl with bits of pineapple and cherries floating in clear syrup. He added a carton of milk and a straw to his tray, then handed his money to the cashier. The woman took his money, studied it in her open palm, then said something Hiroshi didn't understand.

He nodded; he wanted to understand.

She repeated her words, louder this time. Hiroshi wanted to melt into the floor. *What was she trying to say?* Father had checked with the school secretary, who told him that lunch costs two dollars and forty cents. Had Father gotten it wrong? The lady pointed to a machine on the counter that looked like a large calculator and said something else. Then she shook her head and clicked her tongue.

Hiroshi heard Skye's voice next to him. She translated the lunch lady's words, but Hiroshi could barely hear her above the talking and clanging of pots and pans. "She says you didn't give her enough money. It's two forty—you gave her two twenty."

Hiroshi frowned and looked again at the money in her hand. He'd given her two one-dollar bills—that had to be right. Then he'd given her four of those other coins—the second biggest. That was forty cents.

The red-haired boy behind him sighed. Hiroshi felt the heat reach the tops of his ears.

Skye plucked two smaller coins out of Hiroshi's open palm. "Here's twenty more cents." She handed it to the lady, who said something to Skye.

"She says you can pay a month at a time if you want. Then you just enter your student number here." Skye pointed to the machine.

What was his student number? He must have it written down somewhere. "Oh—" Hiroshi began.

But Skye was already heading back to her place in line. He

turned so he wouldn't have to see the exasperation on the other kids' faces. He hated feeling stupid.

Gripping his tray, Hiroshi stepped into the eating area. Where was he supposed to sit? He spotted Ravi at one table, but Ravi wasn't in his regular fifth grade class—only ESL. There were two other tables with signs in the center that read 5TH Grade. But which one was his class? Aside from Skye, he didn't recognize anyone. After ESL class he had spent the rest of the morning trying to be invisible and hadn't paid attention to his classmates' faces. Besides, they all looked the same.

Then he heard Skye's voice coming from behind, chatting with another girl. She stopped beside him, glanced at the girl, then leaned toward Hiroshi and spoke in Japanese.

"Over there." Skye nodded in the direction of their table. But when they got there, Skye and her friend set their trays down in the middle of a bunch of girls, who had taken over the center area. There was an empty seat next to Skye.

Hiroshi glanced over at the boys on either side of the table, but no one seemed to notice he was there. Then that spiky-haired boy passed by. He said something to Skye, and she turned dragon red. The boy sneered at Hiroshi and took a seat at one end of the table. That made Hiroshi's seating choice an easy one: he would sit as far from that boy as possible.

Hiroshi spoke to Skye, but not loud enough so others could hear him. "I'll just sit down there." He could tell something was bothering her, and he was pretty sure it had to do with him. It was obvious that she didn't want other people to hear her speaking Japanese. Hiroshi headed for the other end of the table, opposite the spiky-haired boy, and sat by himself. He couldn't speak enough English, so there was no use sitting next to anyone.

The others had already started eating, without even putting their palms together and wishing everyone a good meal. That was okay—it meant he wouldn't have to wait for the last student to be served when all he really wanted to do was dig in.

Hiroshi picked up his fork. He looked from the spaghetti to his fork and back to the spaghetti again. *How am I supposed to eat this?* He studied the other kids out of the corner of his eye. Some twirled their spaghetti around their forks; others just scooped it up and shoveled it into their mouths. Instead of picking up their bowls and holding them close to their chins, they leaned over their trays to eat.

Hiroshi poked the pile of noodles. It jiggled for a few seconds and then was still. He twirled the spaghetti around like he'd seen the others do, then lifted the fork to his mouth. The spaghetti slipped and spilled down the front of his shirt. Wearing a red shirt had been a lucky choice, after all.

Wiping his shirt with a napkin, he glanced sideways to see if anyone had noticed. No one was paying any attention to him. He couldn't decide which was worse—embarrassing himself or not being noticed at all. He tried the fork again, but only managed to get a few noodles into his mouth and sauce on his cheek. He gave up and ate the fruit and bread, but he was still hungry. He picked up his spoon—maybe that would be easier.

It wasn't.

Then he had an idea. He turned his fork and spoon upside-down and held them between his fingers like chopsticks. He lifted the bowl and held it just below his chin. He didn't care if anyone saw him eat this way; he was hungry.

Mrs. Garcia came into the cafeteria and approached the table. She looked at Hiroshi and frowned. Had he done something wrong? She paused next to Skye and said something. Skye stared at her tray and nodded. Mrs. Garcia clapped her hands, then said something to the class. Chair legs scraped against the floor, and the kids sprang to their feet. They pushed in their chairs, gathered their trays, and headed for the trash cans. Hiroshi started to follow.

"Hiroshi?" Mrs. Garcia smiled at him.

"Yes, Teacher?"

"Tomorrow Skye will sit with you."

Hiroshi wanted to say that it wasn't necessary. But how? He didn't have the words to explain that he couldn't exactly hang out with a group of girls. But he didn't want to disagree with the teacher, so he just nodded and joined the others in line.

Mrs. Garcia opened a door, and the other kids rushed out onto the playground. Some ran to grab the swings; others stood in small groups, laughing and talking together. Hiroshi hung back, not sure what to do. If he were at his school in Japan, he'd be one of those running, laughing, savoring his freedom. He'd organize a game of basketball, boys against girls. But not here, not today.

Today he stood alone.

"You can sit with us at lunch tomorrow." Hiroshi turned to find Skye standing next to him, fists on her hips. "I'm sorry about that guy, Hiroshi. I should just ignore him. And so should you. His name is Kevin. And he's a—" Skye looked like she was searching for the right word.

"*Ijimekko?*"

Skye smiled. "In English we say *jerk*."

"Jerk?"

Skye nodded, but by the look on her face, Hiroshi knew he hadn't said it right. "We'll work on that one later," she said.

"Skye!" One of a group of girls was waving in their direction. Skye looked from the group back to Hiroshi. She seemed like she was about to say something, then closed her mouth.

Hiroshi dragged the toe of his sneaker through the dusty gravel. "Your friends are calling you."

Skye turned to the girls then back to Hiroshi. "Okay, then. I'll see you later?"

He nodded. What could he do? Hiroshi shoved his hands in his pockets and walked to a small hill next to the playground. If he closed his eyes, he could pretend he was back at school in Japan. With friends. With chopsticks. And without English.

"Wait!" Skye waved her arms as her feet pounded down the side-walk, her backpack thumping against her back. The school-bus driver must have seen her, because the stop sign swung out from the side of the bus, the red lights flashed, and the doors opened. "Thanks," she said as she bounded up the steps.

The driver did not look happy. "Be on time tomorrow, Skye. Next time I won't wait."

Skye nodded and paused for a moment to catch her breath be-fore heading down the aisle. She'd lost a good ten minutes this morning looking for her homework folder, and she still needed to finish her math. There weren't many empty seats left, but Amber was waving to her from the middle of the bus. Skye scanned the heads to see if Hiroshi had made the bus. There he was—two rows in front of Amber.

He'd made the bus, all right.

Hiroshi was wearing some kind of mask over his mouth and nose, like doctors sometimes did on TV. White elastic looped around his ears, holding the mask in place.

Is this a joke?

"Find a seat, Skye." The bus driver gave her the evil eye in the rearview mirror. "We're running late."

As Skye walked toward Hiroshi's row, she heard the snickers of the kids who had turned to look at him. "What's he got under there?" one boy asked another kid across the aisle.

"Bad breath," answered the second kid, and they cracked up.

Skye ignored them. Hiroshi nodded at her, like wearing a mask was the most normal thing in the world.

"Skye, come on," Amber called. "I've got your seat right here." Skye offered Hiroshi a feeble wave, then moved past him and sat next to Amber. "So what's with Dr. Hiroshima?" Amber whispered.

"It's *Hiroshi*, not Hiroshima. And I have no idea." Skye sighed as more kids turned and whispered about Hiroshi's mask. If he got off the bus with that mask, he'd be the laughingstock of the whole school. She had to warn him.

When the bus finally lurched to a stop in front of the school, Skye saw her chance. "I'll meet you outside," she told Amber, and hurried up the aisle to catch up with Hiroshi. "What are you doing?" she whispered as the line shuffled toward the bus doors. He turned and answered in Japanese, but with the mask hiding his mouth and muffling his voice, Skye couldn't understand a word he said.

"What?" she whispered louder.

"I said I'm getting off the bus."

Skye rolled her eyes. "I can see that. But why are you wearing a mask?"

"I've got a cold."

Now that he mentioned it, he did sound a little stuffed up. But still. "You need a mask for that?"

Hiroshi looked at her as if *she* were the crazy one. "Of course. I don't want to give anyone my cold germs."

60

Well, he did have a point. She followed him down the steps and up the sidewalk.

"Skye, wait up!" Amber stepped off the bus.

"Just a sec." Skye turned to tell Hiroshi that American kids didn't wear masks, but he had gone ahead and was out of earshot.

When Skye reached the classroom, Hiroshi was already seated, organizing his papers. And still wearing that mask. Skye could see some kids whispering and others pointing, but either he didn't notice or he chose to ignore them. She couldn't wait any longer—she had to tell him to ditch the mask, cold or no cold.

But as soon as she sat down, the bell rang and Mrs. Garcia started calling the roll. Skye tore out a piece of paper from her notebook. She had no idea how to write *take off your mask* in Japanese, and she figured Hiroshi wouldn't know the English version. She drew a stick figure wearing a mask, circled it, and then drew a line through it.

She got up to sharpen her pencil and dropped the note onto Hiroshi's desk. But when she came back, he was still wearing the mask. He pointed to her drawing, his eyes showing his confusion.

Skye closed her eyes and shook her head. *How can he not understand?* When Mrs. Garcia went to speak with another teacher at the door, the class broke out in whispers. Skye leaned into the aisle. "Take that off," she whispered in Japanese.

"This?" Hiroshi pointed to his mask.

"Yes, that!"

He looked confused. "But why?"

"Because no one wears them, that's why!"

Hiroshi didn't make any move to take off the mask. "I must be the only one with a cold."

Skye felt like screaming. He looked ridiculous, and he needed to be told. Better to hurt his feelings a little bit now than to have the other kids tease him. "But you look . . ." What was the Japanese word for *ridiculous?* She had no idea. "You look—I mean, the mask looks . . . well, stupid." That wasn't what she wanted to say. If only she could think of the right word in Japanese.

Hiroshi scowled. "It's not stupid. I don't want to cough all over everyone."

"I'm not saying the idea is stupid. Just that it makes you look—"

"Stupid?"

Hiroshi didn't seem to be taking this well. Skye sighed. "No! Not stupid." More like ridiculous. But she couldn't explain that to Hiroshi.

Just then quiet laughter spread throughout the room. Skye looked up. Mrs. Garcia still stood at the door, looking over some papers with the other teacher. In the back of the room, a kid in the last row had taped a white tissue across his mouth and nose. Skye rolled her eyes and shook her head.

When she turned back to Hiroshi, his eyes told her that he'd figured out who everyone was really laughing at. He slipped the elastic from each ear, folded the mask, and slid it into his desk.

Skye sighed. She'd been trying all morning to make him understand, and now he did.

Understanding isn't all it's cracked up to be.

Hiroshi stepped off the school bus and headed up the sidewalk. Angry tears burned his eyes, but he refused to let them fall. Everything was all wrong—this school, this stupid language that he didn't understand and never would. He just wanted to go home. Back to Japan.

"Hey!" Skye's voice came from behind him.

Hiroshi kept walking. Maybe she'd think he hadn't heard her and just leave him alone.

"You dropped your book!"

Hiroshi was surprised to hear her yell in Japanese. It was probably because they were alone at the bus stop, and no one else was around to hear. He turned to see Skye flipping through his copy of *Tim Gets Dressed*.

"Give that back!" Hiroshi snatched the book from Skye's hands. He shoved it into his backpack and yanked the zipper closed.

"Listen, I'm sorry about the mask."

Right. Hiroshi turned and started up the street. Her words were empty—except for the word *stupid*. That word weighed a ton. Fine. He'd go his way, and she could go hers. Just because they were cousins didn't mean he needed her. He'd figure things out on his own.

63

"Those words aren't the important ones, you know."

He slowed. "What?"

Skye caught up and fell into step beside him. "Your book."

Why did that book have to fall out of his backpack? And why did she have to see it? "I'm not stupid, you know. That book is stupid, but I am not." He kept walking.

Skye followed. "I know you're smart." She shook her head. "You don't need those books. They leave out all the important stuff. Most schoolbooks do."

"Like what?" Hiroshi stopped.

"There's the English you learn in school, and then there's real English."

Hiroshi's curiosity snuffed out some of his anger. But not all of it. "So how do I learn real English?"

Skye stepped off the curb. "Leave that to me," she said over her shoulder. Then she crossed the street and headed home.

What is she talking about? Hiroshi shrugged and shifted his backpack from one shoulder to the other. Girls. They didn't make sense in any language.

When he reached his house, Hiroshi opened the front door, slipped inside, then closed the door without a sound. He heard Mother and Grandfather talking in the kitchen. Slouching against the wall, he closed his eyes and listened to Mother talk about her trip to the supermarket. A month ago Hiroshi would never have stopped to listen to such everyday conversation. A month ago this conversation would have been boring. But after a day of wrestling with English, he let the rise and fall of their Japanese words wash over him. It felt like a small miracle to actually understand what people were saying.

64

When he entered the kitchen, Mother and Grandfather were sitting at the table with cups of green tea. He dropped his backpack onto the floor and sank into a chair.

"How was your day?" Mother asked.

"I don't want to go back."

"Is your cold worse?" She put her hand on his forehead. "No fever. Here, have some tea." She lifted the china teapot by its bamboo handle. Hiroshi watched the steam rise as she poured his tea.

"I still don't understand anything. It's like I never even took English lessons before. And I'm tired of eating without chopsticks."

"You could always bring lunch from home, Hiro-chan," Mother said.

Hiroshi thought of the spiky-haired boy and what he would say if he saw Hiroshi's Japanese food and chopsticks. Better to try and blend in with the others.

"Maybe," he said. "I'll think about it." Hiroshi took a sip of tea. "I'm starving." He reached for the plate of sushi rolls.

Mother handed him a napkin. "I am so glad Sorano-chan is there to help."

Right. Hiroshi popped a sushi roll in his mouth.

"The box containing the dragon kite arrived this morning," Grandfather said. "It's in my workshop, but I haven't unpacked it yet. I thought we'd open it together."

Hiroshi stood and grabbed another sushi roll. "Let's go." Seeing the dragon kite again would be like seeing an old friend.

Hiroshi hurried down the stairs. It wasn't until he had reached the bottom step that he realized Grandfather wasn't behind him. He turned to find him gripping the railing, knuckles white, as he placed both feet on each step.

"Are you okay?"

"I am fine, yes. My old legs just need to get used to these steps."

Hiroshi climbed back up the stairs and offered Grandfather his arm.

"Thank you, Hiroshi. But I can do it myself." Hiroshi stayed close to Grandfather, just in case. "I am starting the new treatment at the hospital soon. I will be good as new in no time."

Hiroshi had always trusted Grandfather. But this time he wasn't so sure.

When they reached the bottom of the stairs, Hiroshi glanced at the high, small windows. "There's not much light down here. There's no view, either. Your workshop in Japan was better."

Grandfather looked at the windows and put his hand on Hiroshi's shoulder. "What do you say we open that box?"

Hiroshi peeled off the packing tape as if he were opening a birthday gift. He bent back the box flaps and dipped his hands into the Styrofoam pellets, feeling for the kite. His fingers closed around its bamboo bones, and he gingerly lifted it out of the box, spilling bits of Styrofoam onto the floor. He unwrapped the tissue paper, one layer at a time, until the dragon's face finally appeared. He had almost forgotten the fierce glint of the eyes and the whiteness of the jagged teeth. But it was the magic of the colors that amazed Hiroshi the most. When the kite danced far up in the sky, the dragon appeared to be different shades of red, depending upon the light of the sun. But up close its skin and scales were tiny strokes of color and light—hundreds of lines of black, reds, blues, and greens. Holding the dragon kite in his hands felt like holding a piece of home.

Then he saw it—a rip in the paper near the top of the kite.

"Oh, no!" Hiroshi peered closer. Grandfather ran his fingers over the dragon's four-inch wound. "Can we fix it?" Hiroshi watched the wrinkles deepen across Grandfather's forehead.

"I don't know. We could patch it, but it wouldn't be as strong."

"Would it still fly?"

"Yes, but it might not survive a *rokkaku* battle."

"All that work for nothing."

Grandfather lifted the kite from Hiroshi's hands and set it on the worktable. "Doing something you love is never a waste of time, Hiroshi."

"Moving to America has ruined everything."

"It may seem like that now, Hiroshi. But it won't always be that way. You'll make many more kites in your lifetime. Even better than this one."

"You mean *we'll* make more kites. Together. You and me."

"Perhaps. But you've become an expert kite maker in your own right. You made this kite yourself. You don't need my help anymore, Hiroshi."

"Yes I do. I put the kite together, but you had to remind me what to do. And I'll never paint like you do."

"The picture does not bring the kite to life; it is the design of the bamboo bones and paper skin that make it fly. I began painting kites sixty years ago." He pointed to the dragon. "Do you think I could paint like this when I was a boy?"

Hiroshi eyed the medallion that hung from the chain around

67

Grandfather's neck. No bigger than a quarter, the medallion's worn inscription was barely legible after all these years. Grandfather had been Hiroshi's age when he had won it, the youngest *rokkaku* champion in his village. As long as Hiroshi could remember, Grandfather had never taken the medallion off.

"What's it like to win?" Hiroshi asked.

"Winning one thing can mean losing something else."

"But you've never lost." Hiroshi took the medallion between his fingers. "You're the best there is."

Grandfather took the medallion from Hiroshi and tucked it back into his shirt. "This medallion does not represent winning, Hiroshi. It is a reminder of the value of humility."

Hiroshi started to ask what he meant, but the faraway look in Grandfather's eyes told him not to ask any more questions. Whenever he'd asked about the medallion in the past, Grandfather always managed to change the subject.

"You have talent, Hiroshi. What you lack is patience. But that, too, will come with time. You'll see."

Hiroshi wasn't so sure. "You can teach me patience. I'll learn from you."

"You must find patience within yourself. I won't always be here to help you. Some things you will need to learn on your own."

But Hiroshi didn't want to learn on his own. "We'll always make kites together, Grandfather."

But even as he said the words, Hiroshi knew they couldn't be true.

"Tsuki-san, please count the number of animals in the picture."

"Yes, Sensei." Skye still couldn't get used to being called by her last name. She breathed in, then let her cheeks puff as she blew the air out. The dramatic sigh didn't buy her enough time—if she were to take as many deep breaths as she needed to think of the right answer, she'd hyperventilate before getting a word out. Come to think of it, hyperventilation wouldn't be too bad. If Skye passed out on the floor, Kumamoto Sensei would naturally have to move on to the next student, right?

Kumamoto Sensei waited, her frown deepening as each second ticked by.

Skye rose and stood beside her desk. *Think. Numbers. Animals.*

Why couldn't the Japanese have come up with one system of numbers, like in English? It wasn't fair to have different sets of numbers for counting different things. Skye had memorized the numbers she needed to count money. And soccer goals. And even long objects, like pencils or forks. But counting animals was a whole different matter.

She stared hard at the picture of rabbits at the front of the room. They were cute. But those cute fluffy tails and pink noses

69

seemed to taunt her in little singsong voices: *You can't count us! You can't count us!*

Skye imagined kicking a soccer ball right at them. Not hard enough to hurt them, just enough to scatter them so they'd run and hide in the bushes and she wouldn't have to count them. Bowling for bunnies.

She took another breath. Small animals. That had to be the number set she needed.

"*Ip-piki, ni-hiki, san-biki, yon . . . yon-biki?*"

Kumamoto Sensei held up her hand, like it was too painful to hear anymore.

Then Skye realized her mistake. "*Yon-hiki!* Not *biki*. That's it—*yon-hiki*."

"*Hai*," said Kumamoto Sensei. "Yes, that is correct if you are counting small animals."

Okay, thought Skye. *Rabbits are small animals*. She continued counting: "*Go-hiki, rok-piki—*"

Kumamoto Sensei was nodding, but held up her hand again. "I am afraid that is incorrect, Tsuki-san. You may be seated."

It was the nodding that always threw Skye off. Whenever an answer was right, there was nodding. When an answer was wrong—more nodding. Talk about confusing.

"Who knows the number set we must use when counting birds and rabbits?"

Everyone's hands shot up. Birds and rabbits? So there was *another* set of numbers for birds and rabbits? But they were small animals, weren't they? Unless Japan had mutant strains of rabbits and birds. Maybe they were huge in Japan, and people rode them around.

70

Kumamoto Sensei called on another kid two years younger than Skye. Figured. Most of the kids were younger than Skye by at least a year.

"Kurahone-san?"

A petite girl with a shiny braid down her back stood beside her desk. In a clear voice, she recited: "*Ichi-wa, ni-wa, san-wa . . .*"

So it was *wa*. Who knew? Not Skye, obviously.

With each syllable, Kumamoto Sensei's smile widened, and the nodding kept getting faster. "*Hai!* Well done, Kurahone-san."

Maya Kurahone—the third grader—sat down, somehow managing to look smug and humble at the same time. One of those "I can't believe I got all the answers right!" looks, when she must have known all along that she'd said the right thing.

Oh, please.

Kumamoto Sensei flashed another picture on the screen, this time of a group of people. Skye raised her hand—she knew this one! But Kumamoto Sensei's gaze skipped over her and on to the next student. Skye felt like slumping in her seat, but that wasn't allowed. So she slumped in her mind instead.

Skye wanted to blame her dad for not speaking to her more in Japanese—but she knew it was her fault, too. She and her dad used to have fun playing games and watching movies in Japanese. But then she kept slipping more and more English words into Japanese sentences whenever she couldn't remember words or rules. Or numbers for birds and rabbits.

These other kids all studied a bazillion hours a week, like learning Japanese was the most important thing on earth. Most of them had come from Japan a year or two before, and their parents wanted them to keep up their Japanese.

Skye's Japanese hadn't been "up" since she was little. She felt like she was climbing a huge hill, and already she was out of breath. She'd never catch up. She probably should have been with the first-grade class, but the school's director must have figured that Skye wouldn't fit in those tiny desks. So there she was, stuck with a bunch of third and fourth graders who knew way more Japanese than she did.

Skye tapped her pencil eraser on her paper, thinking. She had to get out of this class. But to get out, she had to pass the exams.

One on grammar. *Tap, tap,* went her pencil.

One on Japanese history. *Tap.*

One on calligraphy. *Tap, tap, tap.* She actually didn't mind calligraphy. *Tap, tap.*

One on reading. *Tap.*

And one on speaking. The dreaded oral exam. *Taptaptaptaptap . . .*

Skye realized the room had fallen silent. Except, of course, for her tapping pencil. Keeping her chin lowered, she looked up. Everyone was staring at her. At her pencil.

"*Gomen nasai.*" Her shoulders drooped as she mumbled her apology, and she set her pencil on her desk. Kumamoto Sensei gave a quick nod, then moved on. Skye breathed again. If nothing else, Japanese class was good for learning how to take deep breaths. Too bad there wouldn't be a test on that.

Kumamoto Sensei announced the break, then left the room. The other kids all pulled out their *o-bento* containers. Skye took hers out of her desk. Her dad had bought this one for her online. He'd said it was like the ones the kids had in Japan. Maybe it was, but Japanese school was the only place where she'd dare show her face with this *o-bento* box. She'd been hoping for one with soccer balls on it or something. But no. It was pink. With Hello Kitty grinning at her.

She wasn't the only one with Hello Kitty—half the girls had *o-bento* boxes like hers, or with some other equally cutesy designs. The boys had boxes with superheroes—always Japanese, and always looking like they'd just stepped out of some manga comic book.

But there was one difference between Skye's *o-bento* box and the others'—the contents. She lifted the lid, revealing four inner compartments just like the others. Not like the others, hers were filled with pretzels, chunks of pineapple, and a Fruit Roll-Up. The other kids had things like sushi rolls, rice rolls, hard-boiled eggs, and some unidentifiable stuff.

It wasn't like Skye hated Japanese food. Not all of it, anyway. She used to eat it all the time when she was little. Back then her dad cooked a lot more often. But that was when he'd worked from home as a consultant. Now he didn't consult the recipe books anymore—he worked in an office. So her mom did most of the cooking, and it wasn't Japanese food. Mom's specialties were the regular stuff—American food.

Skye watched the other kids with their chopsticks and listened to their chatter—all of it in Japanese, of course. Most of them spoke pretty good English, but if Kumamoto Sensei overheard them speaking it, they'd get marked down for their daily participation grade.

"Sorano?" It was Maya, the one-braid wonder who could talk circles around her any day.

"Mmm?" Skye was thankful that her mouth was full. She couldn't make any grammar blunders while she was chewing, could she?

"Do you want to join our study group? We meet at my house

73

this afternoon, then we rotate so each week we will be at a different person's house."

A study group? Skye and Lucy used to do homework together sometimes. They'd usually end up doing more talking than studying. But sitting around speaking in Japanese with Maya and the others was not Skye's idea of a good time.

Skye forced a bite of pineapple down her throat. "Um, *arigato*, Maya." Skye was about to shake her head before remembering that was a no-no. So she nodded like she was about to say, "Why, yes. A study group would be just lovely." Nodding felt unnatural, like she was lying or something. Actually, she was about to lie; nodding was the least of it. "You see, my cousin just moved here, from Japan."

Maya looked at Skye blankly.

Skye kept going. "So we're going to be studying together. I mean, he'll be helping me out, you know. I won't be helping him, since he already knows Japanese. Being that he is Japanese." She laughed at her own lame joke, but Maya apparently didn't see the humor.

"We are Japanese, too." Maya looked confused.

"Right, I know that. But he just came from Japan. And we live in the same neighborhood and everything." *Couldn't this girl just take no for an answer?*

"Yes, okay." With that Maya turned to another kid. They started chatting, and Maya scratched something off a list she had on her desk. It was official, then—Skye was off the A-list. Not that she cared.

As she finished the rest of her snack, Skye wished Amber were there. Or one of her other teammates. Then she could laugh and

74

joke about the mere idea of having a Japanese study group right after class. They could talk soccer instead of *kanji*.

Skye thought of Hiroshi. *This must be how he feels at school.* At least Skye understood most of the conversation around her, even if she couldn't speak as well as the others. Or write. Or count, apparently. But what would it be like not to understand at all? And to not be able to say even the basic stuff?

Skye thought of Hiroshi's book that had fallen from his backpack the other day at the bus stop—*Tim Gets Dressed.* Ugh. Skye's Japanese book was hard to read, but at least she had the same book as everyone else. Then again, she *was* in a class with mostly third graders. No, she decided Hiroshi's situation was a million times worse. He needed to learn real English, and she would be the one to teach him.

As Skye packed up her *o-bento* box and Kumamoto Sensei came back into the room, an idea began to grow inside of Skye. By the time she walked out the door at dismissal, she had a plan in place. A plan to help Hiroshi.

寛〇

Hiroshi discovered the folded-up paper sticking out of his pencil box on Monday morning before the first bell. He scanned the room to see if anyone was watching him, but no one was.

Hiroshi unfolded the paper and was surprised to see Japanese writing mixed with English:

> Skye's English Tip #1
> Word of the Day 今日の言葉: SUCKS
> Definition: When something is bad, you say "That sucks." If something is really bad, then it "totally sucks."
> Example: It totally sucks when you can't join the soccer team because your parents make you go to Japanese school on Saturday mornings, which is when the All-Star soccer games are.

Hiroshi blinked. *Sucks* would definitely be useful. In fact, it was the perfect word to describe what was coming—Grandfather's first treatment. Hiroshi glanced at the clock. In twenty-five hours and thirty-seven minutes, Grandfather would be waiting in the hospital, probably wearing one of those thin gowns, not knowing what was going to happen. Would he be scared? Hiroshi had never seen Grandfather scared.

In twenty-five hours and thirty-six minutes, Hiroshi would be scared, sitting here in school, thinking of Grandfather. *Skye has it wrong—missing out on a soccer team doesn't suck. Cancer is what totally sucks.*

The bell rang, and Skye took her seat. He glanced at her, smiling his thanks, and she nodded.

Hiroshi made his way through the math worksheet, waiting for nine o'clock. But at 9:05 Mr. Jacobs still hadn't come through the door to pick him up for ESL. Hiroshi double-checked his math. 9:10. Still no Mr. Jacobs.

"Mrs. Garcia?" a voice filtered through a loudspeaker in the ceiling.

"Yes?" Mrs. Garcia answered.

"Mr. Jacobs will be late today. He'll pick up his students when he arrives."

"Thank you, Ms. Baca." Mrs. Garcia stopped by Hiroshi's desk and leaned down. "Did you understand, Hiroshi? Mr. Jacobs will be here soon." Hiroshi nodded. Mrs. Garcia glanced at the paper on his desk. "Do you have an ESL assignment to work on while you wait?"

"Yes, Teacher." Actually, Hiroshi had finished his assignments the night before, but he couldn't just sit there and do nothing. There was no way he was going to pull out his first-grade books in front of everyone.

Mrs. Garcia began the reading lesson for the rest of the class. Hiroshi tried to follow her words, but they all ran together. Then he had an idea. He flipped his ESL notebook over, turned it around, and opened to the last page. This would be a good place to write the new English word Skye had taught him. He began to copy her English tip into his notebook.

"*Psssst!*"

Hiroshi turned. Skye was looking at him out of the corner of her eye and shaking her head. Hiroshi shrugged. *What is she trying to tell me?* She looked back and forth from the paper to Hiroshi, eyes narrowed and shaking her head again, faster this time.

"Hiroshi?" Mrs. Garcia called. Hiroshi jumped, and Skye's eyes snapped back to the front of the room. "It's time for ESL." Mr. Jacobs stood in the doorway and waved. Hiroshi gathered his things and followed him to class.

When everyone was seated in the ESL room, Mr. Jacobs turned to the group. "Sorry I was late today, everyone." He picked up a whiteboard marker. "I ride my bike to school. How many of you ride bikes?" A few kids raised their hands. Mr. Jacobs drew a picture of a bicycle on the board. Hiroshi wished he rode his bike to school, like he had in Japan.

"When I was on my bike, a truck passed me." Mr. Jacobs drew a stick figure on the bike and tapped it with the marker. "That's me." Then he drew a truck. He pointed to the weather chart near the calendar. "What's the weather like today?"

"Rain," someone said. Mr. Jacobs nodded and motioned Ravi to the front. Ravi chose a paper raindrop from a basket and taped it to the chart.

Mr. Jacobs drew a puddle between the bike and the truck. "The truck drove through the puddle. Splash!" He spread his arms and looked down at his trousers. "I got all wet, and had to go home and change." A murmur ran through the class. Poor Mr. Jacobs.

Hiroshi snuck a peek at the last page in his ESL notebook, then closed it. He raised his hand. Now was his chance to make up for the *shoes* mistake; he would show Mr. Jacobs what a good English student he was.

"Yes, Hiroshi?"

Hiroshi cleared his throat. "I am sorry, Teacher." His voice was loud and clear. "That totally sucks."

Mr. Jacobs' eyebrows raised like two question marks. Then he threw his head back and laughed—the kind of laugh that came from his belly. Had Hiroshi made a mistake? He flipped to the back of his notebook again. No, he'd gotten the words right; maybe it was his pronunciation. He closed his notebook and eyed Mr. Jacobs, who was now biting his bottom lip and wiping a tear from his eye with his knuckle.

"Hiroshi, where did you learn that?"

Hiroshi felt his cheeks burning. "I say it wrong?"

"No, Hiroshi." Mr. Jacobs had snuffed out the last of his laughter, but his eyes still twinkled. "It's just that . . . well, it's the kind of thing you say on the playground, not in the classroom."

"Oh."

Hiroshi should have never listened to Skye.

"You weren't supposed to say it to a *teacher!*" Skye said in Japanese as they stepped off the bus and made their way up the sidewalk.

"You didn't *tell* me I wasn't supposed to say it to a teacher!" Hiroshi shot back. "Now I have insulted him, and everyone laughed at me."

Skye sighed and placed her hands on her hips. "You didn't

insult him. He gets that you're learning English and you just said the wrong thing." She shook her head like this had all been Hiroshi's fault. "Okay, fine." She swung her backpack around and let it plop at her feet, then leaned over and unzipped a small pouch in the front.

"What are you doing?" Hiroshi asked.

"Hold on." She dug through the pouch and came up with broken pencils, a half-eaten sandwich, and a small notebook. "Aha!" She pulled out another folded piece of paper, just like the one she had given Hiroshi earlier.

"Oh, no—not another one. I don't need your English lessons." Hiroshi started to walk away.

"Oh, yes, you do. Believe me." She picked up one of the broken pencils. "I have an idea." Skye unfolded the paper and wrote something at the top. "Here." She thrust the note at him.

He stepped forward and snatched it from her hand. "What did you write this time?"

"Look at the top." Skye replaced the pencils, sandwich, and notebook, zipped up the pouch, and flung her backpack over her shoulder. She poked the paper where she had drawn the letter "A" with a circle around it.

"What does it mean?" Hiroshi asked.

"A is for adult. If you see that, it means you can say it in front of adults."

"And if it's *not* for adults?" Hiroshi could hear his voice rising. "Like 'totally sucks' is *not* for adults?"

"Then the *A* will have a line through it. Got it?"

"Fine." Hiroshi looked at the rest of the words on the page:

Ⓐ Skye's English Tip #2
Word of the Day 今日の言葉: CLUELESS
Definition: Knowing absolutely nothing about something
Example: When someone tugs at the corner of his eyes
and says, "Hey, are you Chinese?" you say, "What are
you—clueless?"

Hiroshi frowned. Why would anyone mistake him for
Chinese? But when he looked up to ask, Skye had already crossed
the street. Hiroshi decided he was definitely clueless about everything in America—especially Skye.

空

Skye tossed her backpack at the foot of the stairs and hoped there was something good in the fridge.

"Is that you, sweetheart?" her mom called. Skye found her mom sitting with her laptop at the kitchen table. "How was school?"

"Fine. I guess. Do you have another project due?"

Her mom nodded. "How are things going for Hiroshi?"

"Good." She looked over her mom's shoulder. "Are these the plans for the new library?"

"Mmm. It's coming along nicely." Her mom loved to talk architecture, and Skye hoped she could steer her away from the subject of school and Hiroshi. But her mom shut her laptop and swiveled to look at Skye. "What happened?"

"What do you mean?" Skye grabbed a banana from the bowl on the counter.

"At school. You seem distracted. How is Hiroshi doing?"

Skye shrugged. "I'm starting to teach him some American slang."

Her mom laughed. "That'll be useful as he makes friends. What a great idea."

Skye didn't explain that the English tips were her way of making up for everything. She should have told that kid to stop

82

making fun of Hiroshi's mask. She should sit with him at lunch. And she should have told him not to say "That totally sucks" in front of a teacher. Now he was so embarrassed that he'd probably never speak English again. She peeled her banana and took a bite.

"I'm sure it has to be hard for him—a new place, not understanding the language, missing his friends." Her mom reached out and squeezed Skye's hand gently. "He's so lucky to have you helping him."

Skye looked at her shoes. "Yeah, I guess."

Her mom stood and headed toward the sink. "You don't give yourself enough credit," she said over her shoulder.

Oh, yes she did; she took all the credit for not helping Hiroshi more. "I have to start my homework."

"Homework can wait."

"What?" *That's a new one.*

"Your grandfather called and invited you to the park today. He and Hiroshi are going to fly their kite."

Fly their kite? Hiroshi probably wouldn't want her there. And the thought of speaking first-grade Japanese to her grandfather? "I think I'll pass. I've got a lot of homework."

Skye's mom cocked her head. "Are you sure there's nothing wrong?"

"I'm sure."

"Well, good, because you have to go."

"But I just said—"

"You can do your homework later. Your grandfather starts his treatment tomorrow, and we don't know how it will go, or how he'll feel from here on out." She gave Skye a gentle push toward the door. "Go on. It'll be fun."

Skye sighed. She'd left Hiroshi to fend for himself at school. She wouldn't be able to carry on a conversation with her grandfather in Japanese without sounding ridiculous. And she hadn't flown a kite since she was seven.

Yeah, she was in for a fun time, all right.

Skye hung back once she spotted them. She had parked her bike at the racks near the foot of the hill and stood to watch for a few minutes. The kite was not at all what she'd expected. Instead of a diamond shape, this kite was a hexagon, the sides longer than the triangle-shaped top and bottom. Instead of the usual beach-ball colors, there was a dragon design that seemed to change colors as it traveled across the sky—first a deep red, then a hint of purple, and even some shimmering green. The kite wasn't in the shape of a dragon, of course, but it looked so real—beautiful and terrible, its scales glinting in the sun. It looked like a hexagon-shaped window had been cut out of the sky, and the dragon was staring down at her from some other world.

Her eyes traveled down the string to where her grandfather and Hiroshi stood. She had never seen either one of them look this happy. Not like she'd known them for all that long. Come to think of it, she didn't really know them at all, did she? The two laughed and talked and grinned into the wind, pointing every once in a while to the kite at the top of their string.

Skye winced when she thought about how she'd basically ignored Hiroshi at school. She hadn't meant for things to turn out that way; they just had.

"Sorano-chan!"

Skye realized she'd been staring at the kite again, and that her grandfather had called her name. Her Japanese name. She waved and saw Hiroshi's smile slide off his face. She wanted to turn around, hop on her bike, and pedal all the way home. But her grandfather was beckoning with a gentle smile, like part of that hill belonged to her, too. She trudged up the path, making a list of Japanese kite-flying words in her head. Kite, wind, string . . . that was about it.

"Sorano-chan, how lovely to see you." Her grandfather looked younger than he had last week. Maybe it was the smile.

"Thank you, Grandfather. Um . . . good to see you, too." That wasn't right. Was it? Her Japanese didn't sound formal enough, but Skye couldn't think of another way to say it. "Nice kite." Skye searched her memory for something more. "I mean, the kite is a thing of great beauty." There. That sounded pretty formal, didn't it? Skye thought she saw Hiroshi smirk, but maybe it was just the way he was squinting in the sun.

"I am glad it pleases you, Sorano-chan." Her grandfather smiled at her. She certainly wasn't Maya the Japanese Wonder, but he didn't seem to mind.

"Grandfather and I made the kite," Hiroshi said, glancing at Skye over his shoulder.

She looked at the dragon. "Oh my gosh, you *made* that?"

Grandfather laughed. Hiroshi didn't. "I put it together, and Grandfather painted it."

Her grandfather nodded toward the kite. "Would you like to try, Sorano-chan?"

"Oh, I can't paint. And I've never made a kite. It looks hard."

He smiled. "I meant would you like to try to fly the kite?"

85

Skye saw Hiroshi's shoulders stiffen, so she took a step away from him. "Actually, it's been ages since I've flown a kite. I wouldn't want to crash it."

Grandfather's eyes crinkled when he smiled. "Do not worry. Hiroshi will see to it that nothing happens to the dragon kite."

Hiroshi offered her the reel only after Grandfather nodded. Should she take it? She could see that Hiroshi didn't trust her with the kite. She didn't trust herself with it, either.

Grandfather laughed. "You two look so serious! Go on, Sorano-chan. The dragon does not bite. Hiroshi, show your cousin how the dragon prefers to be handled."

Hiroshi handed the reel to Skye with both hands. The reels she'd remembered had all been plastic, brightly colored, with a handle for holding and an end for wrapping the string. But this reel was a work of art. The smooth, shiny wood had a rectangular prism shape with a handle on each end. Twin dragons were carved on the sides, their tails winding around the handles.

"Did you make this, too?" Skye looked from Hiroshi to Grand-father.

"Yes, many years ago," Grandfather answered. "But I did not do the carving."

Hiroshi looked at Grandfather. "Who did?"

"First Uncle."

Hiroshi's eyes widened.

Skye was still trying to figure out who First Uncle was when Hiroshi turned to her. "Your father carved this? I never knew he was a wood-carver."

Skye stared at Hiroshi. "My father?" There must be some mistake. She looked back at the dragon reel. "*My* father made this?"

But before anyone could answer, Skye felt a tug on the line and looked up. The dragon kite had tipped sideways and was now starting to fall.

Skye gasped. "Oh, no! The dragon!"

Hiroshi looked worried and reached for the reel. But Grandfather placed his hand on Skye's shoulder. "Give it more line." Skye shook her head and tried to give the reel to Grandfather, but he gently pushed it back toward her. "More line, Sorano. Unwind it a bit, then let the dragon pull as much line as he needs."

It didn't feel right to give a falling kite more line, but what did she know? She prayed she was doing it right. "Like this?"

"Just like that." Grandfather nodded. "I can tell the dragon approves of you." Skye could hear the smile in his voice. Sure enough, the dragon started to climb.

"Hold him there, Sorano-chan. That's just fine."

Skye tightened her grip on the handles, and the dragon stopped its climb. She felt the dragon's energy travel from his perch at the top of the sky, down the line, through the reel, and right into her fingers. She shuddered to think what would have happened if the dragon had fallen. Best not to press her luck.

"That's enough for now. Thank you." Skye handed the reel back to Hiroshi, who took it without a word.

"You are a natural, Sorano. Like Hiroshi. And your father."

"My father flew kites, too?"

Grandfather squinted into the sun, tracking the dragon. "He used to be one of the best."

"He never told me. I didn't know he liked flying kites."

"He won several *rokkaku* battles."

"*Rokkaku?* What's that?"

87

Hiroshi spoke up. "It's kite fighting. When you try to make other kites fall from the sky. The kite that's left flying is the winner."

"How do you do that?"

"There are three ways." Hiroshi sounded like maybe he'd forgotten he was mad at Skye. "You can cut your opponent's line, tip his kite, or block its wind—that's the most difficult move."

"Can you teach me?"

Grandfather looked at the gray clouds that were moving in. "It will rain soon. We will begin with a *rokkaku* lesson next time."

Next time. Skye was about to ask what time tomorrow, and then she remembered. Watching the easy way Grandfather pulled in the line as Hiroshi wound it up with the reel, it didn't seem like Grandfather was sick and that tomorrow was treatment day.

Before, this grandfather had been some distant relative she didn't know. Then he was someone who was coming here to ruin her chance to play on the All-Star team. Now he was Grandfather, who was gentle and didn't seem to mind her rusty Japanese. Grandfather, who could fly a kite, and trusted her to fly one, too. Who had taken a brush and some paint and turned a kite into a dragon.

Hiroshi and Grandfather walked Skye home. When they got to her door, her dad was sitting on the porch.

"It looks as if you have a natural flier here, my son."

Skye's dad smiled. "I should have taught her years ago."

Skye wondered why he hadn't. "Grandfather showed me the reel that you carved."

"The reel?" Skye's dad stood.

Hiroshi held it out. "Grandfather told us you carved this."

88

Skye's dad took the reel in both hands. He looked at Grandfather, eyes bright. "You've kept this?"

Grandfather nodded. "Of course. It is the only reel I ever use." Skye's dad nodded and gently handed the reel back to Hiroshi. Grandfather put his hand on Hiroshi's shoulder. "We should be going now. We will talk tomorrow." Skye felt a pang of envy. Hiroshi was lucky that Grandfather lived with his family.

"Thank you, Hiroshi. Thank you, Grandfather. I had a great time." Grandfather smiled, but Hiroshi only nodded. He looked as worried as Skye felt. As they walked away, Skye stood with her dad's arm around her shoulders. "I hope this treatment works."

He squeezed her shoulder. "Me, too."

It had to work. Skye had just found Grandfather, and she wasn't about to let him go.

Hiroshi slid the spelling test under his notebook before anyone could see the D at the top. He'd spelled *pear, pair,* and *pare* right, but he'd mixed up the meanings. Same thing with *to, too,* and *two.* He couldn't remember the differences among them. He'd studied, even if Mr. Jacobs probably didn't think so. But with Grandfather's first treatment yesterday, homophones—or was it homographs? Homonyms? Whatever they were, they'd been the last thing on Hiroshi's mind. *Why did English have to be so confusing?*

"Hiroshi, may I see you, please?" Mr. Jacobs was at his desk while the others worked on the new list of words. Maybe Hiroshi was in trouble because he hadn't started the assignment yet.

Ravi flashed Hiroshi an encouraging smile. But he hadn't seen Hiroshi's spelling grade.

Hiroshi reached Mr. Jacob's desk. Pointing at the grade book, Mr. Jacobs shook his head. Hiroshi looked at the row of letters next to his name: A, A, A, C, C, D.

"Hiroshi, what is happening?" Hiroshi looked away from those letters that spelled failure. Mr. Jacobs went on. "You asked for more of a challenge." Hiroshi nodded, remembering how easy the first two spelling lists were. When he had asked for harder words, Mr. Jacobs had seemed hesitant. But when Hiroshi had earned another

A, Mr. Jacobs had seemed pleased. Then came the two C's, and now the D.

"Would you like easier words, Hiroshi? I don't want to push you too fast." Hiroshi did not remember Mr. Jacobs pushing him. Except for high fives, Mr. Jacobs had never laid his hands on any students. Did American teachers push students who got bad grades?

Hiroshi glanced at the letters again. He hadn't been studying as much as he should have lately. But he would change that. "I want harder words. I can do it."

Mr. Jacobs frowned. "How can I help, Hiroshi?" American teachers were strange—first Mr. Jacobs threatened to push him, and now he was offering to help. But Mr. Jacobs couldn't help. Not unless he could make Grandfather better.

"I will study more, Teacher."

Mr. Jacobs sighed. "Okay, Hiroshi. We'll try once more. But if your grades don't improve, I'll have to give you the same list as the other students."

Hiroshi nodded. He would try harder. Mr. Jacobs had said to write the words and their definitions three times each. Three times was not enough. He would write them twenty times each. He wanted to learn English; it was just taking so long.

No wonder America and Japan were on opposite sides of the world; English and Japanese were opposites, too.

"Grandfather! You're awake!" Hiroshi had raced all the way home from the bus stop.

"Yes, it was about time I got out of that room." After two days

91

on his futon, Grandfather finally seemed back to normal. He looked a little tired around the eyes, but Hiroshi knew Grandfather would feel better with a kite string in his hands.

Hiroshi grinned and dropped his backpack at the foot of the steps. "Let's go to the park!"

"Hiro-chan, is that you?" Mother came into the front hall and eyed his backpack. He knew what she was about to say, but now wasn't the time for homework; it was time for flying kites.

"Grandfather and I are going to the park. We'll be back soon." He started up the stairs to get the kite from his room.

"Homework must be done first, Hiroshi."

"But Grandfather is finally feeling better! We have to go right away."

Grandfather chuckled. "I am not going to disappear, Hiroshi. I will drink some tea with your mother while you do your work, and then we will go."

Hiroshi knew there was no use arguing with Mother, especially with Grandfather on her side. He ran back down the stairs, grabbed his backpack, and raced up to his room. He pulled out his spelling test. Why had he asked Mr. Jacobs for harder words? Now he had to write the words and the definitions, when the other kids only had to write the words. That was because he had insisted on tackling those stupid words that all sounded alike.

He wrote the first word and its definition three times, then glanced at the clock on his desk. Writing everything twenty times each would take too long; he'd get to it later. He copied the rest of the words and definitions three times each, and slipped the paper back into his notebook. He lifted the dragon kite from the hook on his wall, then flew down the stairs.

"Ready!" he called. Grandfather already had his jacket on and was sitting in the front room. He rose when he saw Hiroshi, but he moved as if his muscles were stiff. "Are you okay, Grandfather?"

Grandfather nodded. "I am ready to fly that kite."

Hiroshi wanted to run all the way to the park, but he had to slow his pace to match Grandfather's. It felt like they were wading in Tachibana Bay back home.

When they finally reached the park entrance, Hiroshi's heart thudded. There, at the top of the hill, stood Skye. When she saw them, her face brightened and she waved.

"There she is," Grandfather said. "I hope she hasn't been waiting long."

Hiroshi stopped. "You knew she'd be here?"

Grandfather stopped, too. "Of course. I invited her to join us. Didn't I tell you?"

No, as a matter of fact you didn't, thought Hiroshi. But he could never speak that way to Grandfather. Instead he mumbled, "I must have forgotten."

When Skye was around, everything was different. He and Grandfather didn't talk about the same things. Flying the dragon kite felt like work, not joy. Hiroshi was sure even the dragon didn't want Skye around; that's why it had dipped last time when she'd held the line. She probably would have crashed it if it hadn't been for Grandfather.

"Hiro-chan, are you feeling all right?" Grandfather looked concerned.

"Yes, I'm fine." Now Hiroshi felt guilty for worrying him. He fell into step next to Grandfather. "It's just that—well, I don't know." *How can I tell Grandfather I want it to be just the two of us*

93

again? "It's just that sometimes you and I—we can't talk about the same things with Skye around." Grandfather frowned, but Hiroshi continued. "I mean, she doesn't know any of the people or places we know in Japan, so it might be rude to talk about them in front of her. She might feel left out." *There. That sounded unselfish enough, didn't it?*

Grandfather put his hand on Hiroshi's shoulder. "You know, Hiroshi, you are right." Hiroshi looked down to hide his smile. Now Grandfather would think of a polite way to cut today's flying session short. Maybe Skye would go home early, and he and Grandfather would stay a little later. "Sorano-chan—I hope you have not been waiting long."

"Hello, Grandfather. Hi, Hiroshi. No, in fact I just finished my homework." She pointed to her backpack resting on the bench. "I wasn't sure when you'd get here, so I brought my homework with me and did it here. I just finished."

"What an industrious girl you are, Sorano."

Looking at Skye, Hiroshi knew she hadn't understood *industrious* in Japanese. Maybe he would tell her later. Or maybe not. But Skye must have understood that Grandfather was pleased to see her, because now she was beaming.

"Are you ready for another flying lesson?" Grandfather asked.

"Yes!" Skye looked as if she couldn't wait to get her hands on the dragon.

Grandfather rubbed his hands together. "Wonderful!" He turned to Hiroshi. "What shall you show her today, Hiroshi?"

How about the way home? But Hiroshi knew he couldn't say that. Instead he shrugged. "The launch?"

A clap from Grandfather. "Perfect! Hiroshi is an expert at

launching, Sorano. You can learn a great deal from him if you wish." Grandfather's words filled Hiroshi's chest. Maybe it wouldn't be so bad teaching Skye a thing or two. Just as long as it didn't get to be a habit.

"Are you ready?" Hiroshi eyed Skye. She nodded, her eyes shining with excitement.

Hiroshi studied the clouds that crept across the sky. "There is some wind up there, but not much. On days like this, it's better to have another person to help with the launch."

"Okay— just tell me what I need to do."

He handed the dragon kite to Skye. "Hold it by the frame and point it toward the sky, like this." He angled the kite upward. "Now face into the wind."

Skye turned slightly. The breeze barely lifted her hair from her forehead. "Like this?"

"Good. When I say 'Now,' let it go, and I'll pull it up into the air."

Hiroshi unrolled his line as he backed away from Skye. "But make sure you let go *right* when I say 'now,' or you'll rip the kite."

Skye rolled her eyes and laughed. "I get it, Hiroshi."

Was it his imagination, or had the wind picked up? Hiroshi stopped and turned his back to the breeze. He let the reel unwind for a few more feet, then grasped the line.

"Now!"

Skye let go of the kite and Hiroshi lifted the line until his arm was stretched above him. He shuffled backward, faster and faster, and the dragon climbed higher and higher. The wind took hold of the kite and Hiroshi let out more line, surrendering the dragon to the sky.

"It worked!" Skye ran up to Hiroshi. He nodded, keeping one eye closed to block out the sun. He practiced a few dives and twists with the kite before allowing it to drift higher. He'd half expected Skye to mess up the launch, but he had to admit she'd done a pretty good job. Well, he didn't have to admit it to *her*.

"Nice work, you two!" Grandfather's voice came from the bench behind Hiroshi and Skye.

"Thank you, Grandfather," Hiroshi and Skye said in unison. They glanced at each other, and their smiles faded.

"Hiroshi came up with a good idea on the way over here," Grandfather said.

Good idea? What good idea?

"He said there are many things about Japan that you have not heard of before, Sorano. And people whom you do not know. This is as good a time as any for Hiroshi and me to teach you."

What? First kite-flying lessons, now lessons on Japan? Why does Skye need to know all of that, anyway?

"I would love to hear about Japan," Skye said. Hiroshi looked at the dragon and sighed. There was no way Skye would be going home early now.

Grandfather turned to Skye. "Sorano, is there anything in particular you would like to know?"

Skye nodded, like she'd been thinking of a question all along. "I've been wondering—I mean, I've asked my father, of course— but I'd love to know more about my grandmother."

Grandfather's face softened, and although part of him looked sad, he seemed pleased by the question. "I will tell you a story about when we were young. This is one of Hiroshi's favorites."

96

Hiroshi could barely remember Grandmother, but he'd heard so many stories about her that it felt like he'd known her all his life. "Why don't you bring the dragon down, Hiroshi? This is a story for sitting."

Hiroshi wondered which story it was—he had many favorites. He handed the reel to Skye. "Can you take up the slack with the reel?"

Skye nodded, looking pleased. With Skye holding the reel, Hiroshi was free to pull in the line hand over hand, coaxing the dragon lower. The kite fluttered down the last few feet, right into Hiroshi's hands, as if the dragon wanted to hear Grandfather's story, too.

Grandfather settled in and began. "Your grandmother was a brilliant kite flier."

"She was?" Skye grinned. "Did you teach her?"

Grandfather nodded. "That is a longer story for another time. But her most brilliant move with a kite string was the time she saved her father's farm."

Hiroshi smiled. He knew this story by heart.

"Crows have always been a challenge for farmers. One year in particular the crows seemed to have doubled in number. They were picking away at the seeds in the furrows, and everyone worried there would not be enough food to last the winter. Until your grandmother had a brilliant idea."

"The hawk kite!" Hiroshi grinned.

Grandfather looked up as if he expected to see such a kite overhead. "Your grandmother designed a kite that was shaped like a hawk. When she flew it over her father's fields, the crows stayed away."

"Wow, that was smart," Skye said. "But she couldn't fly the kite all day, could she?"

"With the help of her brother, they mounted the kite on a bamboo pole and put it in the middle of the field. Soon all the farmers wanted one. I helped her make many hawk kites that season, which brought extra income to our families."

Skye beamed. "What else did Grandmother do?"

Grandfather laughed. "We will have to save that for another time. It is getting late." Grandfather looked toward the sun, which was now behind the trees on the other side of the park. "Next time we would love to hear one of your stories, Sorano. Wouldn't we, Hiroshi? I am sure you must have some soccer stories to tell." Hiroshi nodded, looking at his shoes. Grandfather stood. "It is time we walked Sorano home."

As he and Skye got up, Hiroshi heard a sickening *crunch*. Skye looked down; her hand flew to her mouth, and she gasped.

"What?" Hiroshi followed her gaze where the dragon kite was pinned under her feet.

"I'm so sorry!" Skye stepped off the dragon and reached for the kite, but Hiroshi blocked her with his arm.

"Don't touch it!" Hiroshi knelt and cradled the kite in his hands. He stood slowly, as if he were holding a cup filled with water and had vowed not to let a single drop spill. "Look what you did." He wasn't even sure if he had said the words out loud until Grandfather spoke.

"Hiroshi." Grandfather's voice was stern. "It was an accident that can be fixed."

Skye apologized again, but Hiroshi couldn't speak. The sight of the wounded kite and the sound of Grandfather's harsh words drained the strength from Hiroshi's knees. He sank onto the bench with the dragon on his lap, inspecting the damage in the fading light. Bamboo splintered through the ripped paper.

Could this be fixed? When the kite had torn before, Grandfather had worked his magic and mended the tear. But this time? The bamboo pole would have to be replaced, which meant separating the broken pole from the kite, repairing the tear, and then attaching a new pole. He looked at Grandfather for answers, but Grandfather had his arm around Skye's shoulder. Her face was pale. Grandfather gave Hiroshi a look that warned him not to say anything more.

Why was Grandfather feeling sorry for *her?* She was the one who hadn't been careful. She was the one who had broken the kite. And Grandfather was too sick to make another one. This was too much.

Hiroshi stood, tucking the kite under his arm.

"It is time to head home," Grandfather said. Skye nodded, looking miserable.

The walk to Skye's door only took about ten minutes, but it felt like an hour. Hiroshi wished he could cover his ears to block out Skye's apologies and Grandfather's reassurance that they could fix the kite. Before Skye had opened her front door, Hiroshi turned away as he mumbled good night.

"Hiro-chan, you were too hard on Sorano." Grandfather's voice was gentle, but his words cut right through Hiroshi.

"But she ruined the kite!"

"A person's heart is infinitely more important than any object."

Hiroshi wanted to say that the dragon kite wasn't just any object, but he knew he wouldn't be able to keep the anger from his voice. He fixed his eyes on the ground.

"Your grandmother would have loved to see you and Sorano flying the kite together."

All Hiroshi could do was nod. Why did everything always come back to Skye? What Hiroshi needed was more time with Grandfather, without Skye around. Now all he had to do was think of a way to get it.

17
Skye

Skye shut the front door, snuck past the smell of dinner, and headed for the stairs.

"Skye, is that you?"

She knew her dad wouldn't let her sneak upstairs without tasting whatever it was he was cooking. She backtracked and leaned against the kitchen doorframe. Her dad was stirring something in a pot.

"Did you have a good time?" He stopped, took a sip, nodded, then kept stirring.

"I broke the kite, and—" Skye's voice cracked. Her dad took one look at her and set the spoon down. "I ruined everything." Skye took a shaky breath.

"What happened?" Her dad came and gathered her in a hug.

Skye leaned against him. "I accidentally stepped on the dragon kite and broke it."

"Oh, honey. I'm sure Grandfather knows it was an accident."

Skye shook her head. "It doesn't matter. It's broken."

"I've never met a kite your grandfather couldn't fix."

"But Hiroshi thinks it's broken for good—I could tell."

"Nothing's ever broken for good. Come." He led Skye to the

101

stove. He stirred the pot, then held the wooden spoon out, one hand cradled underneath to catch the drips. "Here, taste."

Skye blew on the clear liquid then took a sip. Her eyes stung. "Wow—spicy. What is it?"

Her dad grinned. "I knew you'd like it. It's too spicy for your mother, so I've made a milder version for her." He pointed the wooden spoon at a smaller pot bubbling away on a back burner. "*Negi shio* soup."

Skye had never been a fan of seaweed. She leaned forward and peeked into the pot. Black-green strips churned in the boiling water. Maybe she could just eat the broth and leave the seaweed.

"Dad?"

"Mmm." He was staring into the pot, stirring and sniffing.

"Can I ask you something?"

"Of course."

"Where'd you and mom get my name?"

His spoon kept moving. "What, honey?"

"Sorano. My name. Why did you choose it?"

Her dad smiled. He turned down the heat to simmer and put a lid on the pot, leaving a crack for steam to escape. Then he wiped his hands and leaned against the counter. "Did Grandfather tell you the story?"

Skye shook her head. "He told me Grandmother's hawk kite story."

Her dad laughed. "He must have told that one a million times."

"It sounds like she was pretty smart."

Skye's dad nodded. "She was. You would have loved her, and she would have loved you."

"So how could you just leave them and never go back to Japan?"

Her dad sighed. "It's complicated, Skye."

"That's what you always say. Either that or you tell me it's something I'll understand when I'm grown up. Well, I'm not a little kid anymore, Dad. And I want to know."

He shut off the heat under the soup, and slid the lid completely over the top with a clank. "Let's have a seat." She followed him to the kitchen table.

"First of all, your name."

Skye rested her chin in one hand.

"Your mother and I decided on *Sorano* as soon as we found out we were expecting a girl. It was your mother who first suggested it, actually."

"Mom didn't want me to have an American name?"

Her dad shook his head. "She was adamant that you have a Japanese name. By that point we knew that our life was here, and she didn't want you to forget your Japanese side."

My Japanese side. Until a few weeks ago, Skye had never thought of herself as having a Japanese side.

"You already know Sorano means *of the sky*," her dad said.

Skye nodded—then stopped, as something suddenly clicked. "The kites. You named me Sorano because of the kites, didn't you?"

Her dad chuckled. "You come from a long line of kite fliers, makers, and fighters."

Skye smiled. "Grandfather, of course. And Grandmother."

"And I, too, learned *rokkaku* from my father." Her dad's eyes looked like they were focused on something from a long time ago. "So did my brothers. I even taught your mom a thing or two about kites." He smiled.

"So my name makes sense now."

Her dad nodded. "Your mother said that your name would be one way of passing on your family history."

Skye remembered the day she had announced that she wanted to change her name. Her dad had chaperoned their first-grade class trip to the zoo and had spoken to her in Japanese the whole time. When the other kids overheard, they kept asking her what she was (American), where she came from (America), and how come she spoke Chinese (it's not Chinese; it's Japanese). Then Josh Nesbit had said, "If you're not Japanese, why do you have such a weird name?"

From that moment on, Skye became her American name. Her real name.

Now Skye's dad was studying her, as if reading her thoughts. "Your mother was crushed when you insisted on going by Skye." He smiled. "I told her it was a phase that would pass. Maybe one day it will."

Skye didn't answer. She couldn't just change her name back now. All her friends called her Skye. Did she even want to change it back?

"What will pass?" Skye's mom came in through the garage carrying two bags of groceries.

"Hey." Skye got up to help with the bags.

"Thanks." Her mom planted a kiss on Skye's forehead. "You two look so serious. What were you talking about?"

Skye didn't want to bring up the subject of her name, especially now that she knew how her mom felt about it. "I was just asking Dad why you decided to leave Japan and never go back."

Her parents exchanged glances and her dad nodded. "Why

don't we get dinner on the table, eat, and then we can talk?" her mom said.

Once the groceries were put away, they all sat down to dinner. Skye fished around the floating seaweed to get to the broth, wondering what her favorite dish would have been if her parents had decided to stay in Japan.

"This is delicious, Issei," her mom said, smiling. "You should cook Japanese food more often."

"Thanks." Her dad bit into a rice ball and closed his eyes. "Mmm. I think you may be right."

Skye took a sip of the broth. "Speaking of Japanese food . . ." Skye gave her soup another stir. "And Japan . . ."

Her mom smiled. "Okay, okay. We get the hint." She took a sip of water. "Let's see, where to begin?" She looked like she was thinking it over. "I didn't meet your father's family until after we had decided to get married. They lived on the island of Kyushu, and we lived on Honshu, in Tokyo—about a day's train ride away."

"That part was my fault," Skye's dad cut in. "I should have brought you to meet them long before that."

"No, Issei, it was no one's fault."

"What was no one's fault?" Skye felt like she wasn't even in the room.

Her mom sighed. "Right. Anyway, for whatever reason, I didn't meet your father's family until we had decided to get married. We went down on the train for the weekend so I could meet them."

Skye's dad leaned forward. "This part definitely was my fault. I'd told my parents that I had a surprise for them, one that I couldn't reveal over the phone."

"And Mom was the surprise?"

Her mom nodded. "I was a surprise, all right."

"Since I hadn't been home in so long, I had fallen out of touch with what was happening in the village. My mother was ill, and my family hadn't told me."

"But why?" Skye couldn't imagine. "You would tell me if Mom were sick, right?"

"Of course we would, sweetheart," her dad said. "It was my mother who didn't want to admit that she was sick. She would eventually have to face the facts, of course, but this was still early on in her sickness."

"So what did she have?" Skye didn't have a good feeling.

"She had a different kind of cancer from what Grandfather has, Skye. It was leukemia, cancer of the blood."

"Oh." That sounded horrible.

Her dad sighed. "Your grandmother was not fond of Americans, I am sorry to say. Our village lies across Tachibana Bay from Nagasaki. At the end of World War II, the Americans dropped a terrible bomb on that city, and tens of thousands were killed. Of those who survived, thousands more developed cancer from the bomb's radiation."

Skye had heard of the bomb, World War II, and Pearl Harbor, although she hadn't studied any of it in school yet. Even though none of it was her fault, she felt guilty for what her two countries had done to each other.

"So my grandmother didn't like Americans because of the war. Okay, I get that. But Mom wasn't even alive during that war. How could she not like Mom?"

Her mom smiled and squeezed Skye's hand. "It's a lot more

complicated than that, honey. Your grandmother's older sister developed leukemia shortly after the bomb fell and died soon after. And her older brother, a soldier, was killed in combat."

"So that's why she didn't like Americans."

Her dad looked embarrassed. "That's why. But I didn't think she would hold a grudge once she met your mother and understood how in love we were."

Her parents fell silent, and Skye didn't dare ask another question. Most of the questions jumbled in her head were ones her parents couldn't have answered, anyway—like whether or not her grandmother really would have liked her. Her dad thought so, but Skye wasn't so sure. Would she have minded that Skye was half American?

"When your dad introduced me to his family, they were very polite. I think they may have even thought I was English at first. I hadn't been learning Japanese for very long at that point, so I don't think they could tell what kind of an accent I had."

"So did you tell them you were American? Or did they guess?"

"Your grandfather asked if I missed my family and whether I saw them much. I said that yes, I missed them, but with America being so far away, visiting was difficult." Skye's mom sighed. "And that's when they all knew."

Skye's dad patted her mom's hand. "I remember holding my breath at that moment, hoping—" Her dad shook his head.

"Maybe we would have become friends, if it hadn't been for her diagnosis," Skye's mom said. "It was too recent, and I think it opened up a lot of wounds that just couldn't be mended."

"But what about Grandfather?" Skye couldn't imagine that he would snub her mom, American or not.

Her dad smiled. "He has always been the family mediator—for spats between my brothers, especially. He always made us work out our differences." His smile faded. "But there was nothing he could do this time. He was never rude to your mom, but he stood by my mother's decision that I must choose between them and my future wife. Obviously, I chose your mom." He smiled. "And I've never regretted my choice for a minute."

Skye saw her parents' eyes go teary, and she tried to swallow past the lump in her throat.

"Did you ever call them or see them after that?"

Her dad nodded. "I tried, especially as my mother's health worsened. My father was so devastated by the thought of losing my mother that he did not want to go against her wishes. But I did keep in contact with my brothers—Hiroshi's father in particular."

"Your father was offered a job in Washington, DC, soon after that, and we made the decision to move to the States."

"And my grandmother, she—?" Skye didn't want to finish the question.

"She died about six months later."

"Didn't you go back then?" Skye asked.

"I wanted to go back for the funeral, but all three of my brothers advised against it. Your grandfather was grieving, and they thought my being there would only make things worse. I should have gone. I know that now."

"How do you know?"

"I had a long talk with your grandfather when he first arrived here with Hiroshi's family. He said he had hoped to see me at my mother's funeral. He took my absence as a sign of bad will on my part, and that's why he never opened any of the letters I sent after my mother died."

"So this whole time he thought you were mad at him, and you thought he was mad at you?" Skye couldn't figure out adults sometimes.

Her dad shook his head. "So many years lost because of a misunderstanding."

"And then I came along."

"Yes." Her mom smiled.

"Did they even know about me?"

Her mom nodded. "I sent them your birth announcement and a photo but never heard from your grandfather. Your uncles called, of course. I continued to send your grandfather a photo every year on your birthday, but he never answered."

Her dad cut in. "Meeting you now has been a joy for him, Skye. I know he appreciates how hard you're working in Japanese school so the two of you can get to know each other."

There was that guilt again. Sure, she'd been working hard—so she could play on the All-Star soccer team. Which suddenly didn't seem as important as it was an hour ago.

Skye hugged her parents a little longer than usual. "Thanks for telling me the story."

Her mom nodded. "Thanks for waiting so long to hear it. It was about time we told you."

Time. There was a lot of that to make up.

"It works!" Hiroshi couldn't believe the dragon was back up in the air. He gave the dragon more line, urging it to climb. "We did it!"

Grandfather smiled. "*You* did it, Hiroshi. You fixed the dragon."

"Except for the paint." Hiroshi could still see the dragon's white wound where he'd replaced the *washi* paper.

"We can paint that later this week," Grandfather said. "For now it is enough to know that the dragon can still fly."

Hiroshi felt the cell phone vibrate in his jacket pocket. He didn't want to break his concentration on the dragon, but he knew his parents would be worried if he didn't answer. They'd made him take it along in case Grandfather grew tired and needed a ride home.

"Can you hold the reel, Grandfather?" Hiroshi slipped the phone from his pocket and pressed the answer button. "*Moshi, moshi.*"

"Hiro-chan?" It was Mother. "Skye just left a message for you on the machine."

"What did she want?"

"She didn't say. But she's home now from Japanese school, so she might like to join you and Grandfather in the park. Why don't you give her a call?"

Hiroshi said good-bye to Mother and sighed. Even as he dialed Skye's number, he tried to think of the best way to keep her away from the park.

"Hello?" Skye picked up after half a ring.

Hiroshi stepped away from Grandfather, holding a hand over one ear as if the phone connection were bad. "It's me, Hiroshi. Mother said you called."

"Hey. I'm home from class, and I thought I'd come over and help fix the kite."

Hiroshi watched the dragon flap in the breeze. There was no way he would ever let her touch that kite again. "Um, I fixed it already."

"Wow—that was fast."

"I stayed up last night and worked on it. It turned out okay, I think."

"That's great, Hiroshi. Can we fly it?"

Hiroshi snuck a look at Grandfather and hesitated. Grandfather seemed to be focused on the dragon, but Hiroshi switched to English, just in case. "I . . . I have a test. I must study."

"A test? But today is Saturday. Did Mrs. Garcia say anything about a test?"

"It is for ESL." Hiroshi could almost hear Skye pouting. "A very hard test."

"But you have two whole days to study. Let's fly the dragon kite for just an hour. I'll help you study later."

Grandfather raised a curious eyebrow at the phone.

"I cannot now." Hiroshi took a few more steps away from Grandfather. Not telling Grandfather that Skye was on the phone felt like lying. But he knew Grandfather would only invite her over, and he didn't want her to hear Grandfather's voice and know they were at the hill.

"Hiroshi? Are you still there?"

"Yes. But the kite cannot fly—the glue is still wet."

"Oh."

He heard Skye sigh and for a moment he felt a stab of guilt. "Maybe one other day we can fly the kite."

"Okay. Well, I'm just glad the kite is fixed. And sorry about what happened."

"Yes. No problem."

"Wait! Hiroshi, is Grandfather there? He might want to go to the park."

"Maybe another day," Hiroshi said. Now Grandfather was walking in his direction. "Um, Grandfather is not feeling well." Hiroshi spoke quickly and kept his voice low. "I have to go now. *Sayonara.*" Hiroshi stuffed the phone back into his pocket as Grandfather handed him the reel.

"You were speaking in English." Grandfather sounded proud, which made Hiroshi feel even more guilty. "Was that one of your American friends?"

"Kind of." Hiroshi pretended to study the dragon as it swooped from one pocket of wind to the next. "It was Sorano." He didn't want to tell Grandfather, but since she'd left a message with Hiroshi's mom, Grandfather was sure to find out once they got home.

"Wonderful! Did you ask her to join us?"

Hiroshi bit his lip. "She has soccer practice." She did have soccer practice—sometimes. Just not right now.

112

"She does?" Grandfather sounded doubtful. "She did not mention this." He shrugged. "We can invite her next time."

Hiroshi focused on the dragon for the next twenty minutes, trying to forget about Skye. The dragon flitted from one cushion of air to the next, then parked at the top of its string. It floated, staring down at Hiroshi. Accusing.

Hiroshi couldn't do it. Grandfather would find out about the lie, and then what? Hiroshi dug for the phone in his pocket. He was about to ask Grandfather to take the reel again when he heard him say, "There she is!"

Hiroshi turned and saw Skye standing at the foot of the hill, her bike at her feet. She was looking at them—at him—like someone had slapped her.

When Hiroshi offered half a wave, Skye picked her bike up and turned around. Grandfather looked confused. Hiroshi saw Skye pause, then turn back around. She hopped on the bike and didn't stop pedaling until she'd gained enough speed to carry her clear to the top of the hill. She skidded to a halt, swung her leg over the seat, and leaned the bike against the bench. Without even taking off her helmet, she marched over to where they stood, the dragon now flapping overhead. Hiroshi swallowed hard.

Grandfather went to meet her. "Sorano, I am so pleased that you could join us after all. Was your soccer practice canceled?"

"Soccer practice?"

Hiroshi winced and turned his gaze to the dragon.

"And you, Grandfather? Are you feeling better?"

Grandfather smiled. "Better than ever."

Hiroshi could feel Skye's stare boring into his back, but he didn't dare look at her. "Oh, really?" Her voice was rising. "Better

113

than ever? I thought you weren't feeling well." Hiroshi snuck a look at Grandfather's puzzled face, and then watched as the sarcasm drained right out of Skye. "I am happy that you are well," she said.

"Did you come to fly the dragon?" Grandfather asked.

"The glue's dry?"

Grandfather laughed. "The glue dried hours ago—it is a fast-drying, very strong glue." He smiled at Hiroshi. "While I slept, Hiroshi worked his magic on the dragon. With some touch-up paint, it will be as good as new."

Hiroshi glanced at Skye. Would she give him away?

"Sorano?" Grandfather was waiting. Hiroshi held his breath. He was sure the dragon was holding its breath, too.

"I'd love to fly it, thank you." Skye turned and glared at Hiroshi. He handed over the reel, and glared back. They fought with stares until Skye looked away, up at the dragon. Hiroshi could see it was tugging on the line.

Skye looked panicked and handed the reel to Grandfather. Hiroshi was secretly glad. He was sure that the longer Skye stayed, the more tempted she'd be to tell Grandfather that Hiroshi hadn't exactly told the truth.

"Are you sure you do not want to fly longer?" Grandfather asked as he fed the dragon more line. He glanced at Hiroshi with questioning eyes.

"No, I'll just watch you fly it for now." Skye took off her helmet and dropped it at her feet. No one spoke as the dragon bobbed and weaved, showing off now that it had its audience's undivided attention.

"Sometimes two people are silent in the very moment in which they have the most to say." Grandfather spoke without taking his eyes from the sky.

Hiroshi looked sideways at Skye. Why didn't she just leave? Surely she could see that he didn't want her there. Grandfather finally felt strong enough to fly the dragon, and now here she was butting in again.

"I think I'll rest for a bit on the bench," Grandfather said. "Who would like to hold the reel?"

Neither of them volunteered.

Grandfather raised an eyebrow. "We could reel the dragon in, I suppose, if you two want to stop for the day."

"No!" Skye and Hiroshi said together.

Grandfather laughed. "Good. I was beginning to worry." Hiroshi stepped forward and took the reel. "You might show Sorano how to climb out of a stall." Grandfather closed his eyes, lifting his face to the sun. "The wind has died down. It is a good day to learn the stall technique."

Grandfather sat, leaving Hiroshi and Skye in command of the kite. But now the dragon didn't seem to want to stay in the sky. It tilted and veered off to the left, showing its underbelly where the sun shone through the patched paper. Where Grandfather would have to touch up the paint. Where Skye had crushed it under her foot. The white slash across the dragon's belly—that's why it wasn't flying well.

"Here, hold this." Hiroshi thrust the reel at Skye. He just wanted to get this over with. He saw her hands tighten on the reel. "Hold the ends of the reel, but don't grip; keep your fingers in a loose O." He saw her grip relax. That was better. As the dragon tugged, the reel spun in her hands. Hiroshi held his breath until the dragon finally straightened its path. Now it seemed to be strutting across the sky, as if to say, *See? I was just playing with you all along.*

"Nicely done, Sorano." Grandfather's voice carried from the bench. "Go ahead and set up a stall, Hiroshi. She'll need to learn how to get out of it."

Why did she need to learn that? Hiroshi could tell Skye didn't understand all of Grandfather's words. Hiroshi sighed, then said in an encyclopedia voice loud enough for Grandfather to hear: "A stall is when the wind stops. It can be dangerous because the kite can start to dive. But if you give the kite more line, it should climb back up."

Skye nodded. "Like it did just now."

"Right." Hiroshi could hear the coldness in his voice, but he couldn't help it.

Skye frowned. Then she edged closer to Hiroshi, turning her back toward Grandfather. "Why did you say you'd be studying all weekend?" she said under her breath.

Hiroshi didn't answer. He glanced at Grandfather, but it didn't seem like he'd overheard.

"Why did you say—"

"I heard you." The words flew from his mouth in a loud, angry whisper.

"Why are *you* mad at *me?* You're the one who told a big, fat lie." When Hiroshi didn't answer, Skye kept going. "Two lies—one to me and one to . . ." She nodded over her shoulder. "Grandfather," she finished.

Hiroshi looked back at Grandfather, who seemed intent on

116

following the dragon's progress. Hiroshi closed his eyes for a moment. *Why can't she just go away?* When he opened his eyes again, she was still there, of course, and he was angrier than ever.

"Before we came to America, it was always Grandfather and me flying kites together." Hiroshi lowered his voice. "Now you're always around."

"Always around? What are you talking about?" Skye's voice was rising. "You're the one who always gets to be with Grandfather! He *lives* with you."

"I don't get to be with him all the time. He's either too sick or too tired. Except when you're around." Hiroshi knew his voice was getting louder, too, so he took a breath.

"But you had all that time with him in Japan!" Skye said. "I have the right to get to know my own grandfather before he—" Skye bit off the last word and looked away.

"Hiroshi? Sorano?" Grandfather was walking toward them.

"I have to go." Skye scooped up her helmet, put it on, and clicked the strap closed under her chin.

Good. Let her go.

"Sorano, are you certain you cannot stay?" Grandfather looked concerned. Skye nodded, then hopped on her bike and pedaled away.

Fine. Now he and Grandfather could fly the dragon in peace.

Until Grandfather found out about the lie.

Skye raced down the sidewalk, barely slowing her bike as she turned into her cul-de-sac. She coasted up the driveway, then skidded to a stop. *How dare he? How dare he lie and steal my time with Grandfather?* She stomped up the walk, almost crashing into her dad, who opened the front door and stepped out onto the porch. He looked at Skye and frowned. "What's wrong?"

Skye shook her head. "Nothing."

"Good, because I have some news for you."

"News?" By the grin on his face, it had to be something good.

"I just got off the phone with my brother."

"Hiroshi's father?" Skye folded her arms.

Her dad nodded, still grinning. "We were talking about how hard your Saturday Japanese classes are."

"Dad! I don't want them to know it's hard for me."

"Skye, it would be hard for anyone in your situation."

"In my situation?" Did he mean someone not Japanese enough?

"You know what I mean. I haven't been diligent about insisting you speak Japanese at home, and you're in a class with native speakers."

Was he saying she wouldn't have to take the classes? Now *that* would be good news.

"As it turns out, Hiroshi needs help with English, too."

If she hadn't been so mad, she would have laughed. It was obvious Hiroshi hadn't been studying for any big ESL test, that was for sure.

"So we decided it would be a great idea if you tutored each other."

Skye blinked. "I don't really think that's a good idea, Dad."

"You're right—it's not a *good* idea. It's a *great* idea!"

She shook her head. "I don't need a tutor. And I'm already helping Hiroshi with English."

"You do need some help, Skye. And I'm sure Hiroshi would be happy to have more help with English. You'll make a great teacher."

"*Will?* That sounds like it's all decided. Have you told Hiroshi about this? I'm sure he—"

"It's all settled, Skye. Come on, don't look so down about it. You'll improve your Japanese, pass your exams, and then you'll be free to play on the All-Star team this summer."

Her dad looked triumphant, like playing the All-Star card would clinch the deal. Sure, Skye still wanted that spot on the team. But was it worth being forced to tutor Hiroshi? Was it worth accepting his help in Japanese?

"Besides," her dad added, "it'll be a great way for you to get to know each other better."

No, thank you, thought Skye. She already knew enough to know that Hiroshi was selfish and rude. Then Skye thought of something. "Where would we have to meet?"

Her dad shrugged. "I suppose you could either meet here or at his house."

119

Maybe if they met at Hiroshi's house, she'd get to see Grandfather more often. Skye sighed. "Okay, then. I guess I'll do it."

"I'm proud of you, honey. I know you'd do anything to get to play on that team, and here's your chance."

Skye nodded. "Right. I'll do it for the team."

Hiroshi had been waiting two straight days for the sun. The rain had started as harmless drizzle on the day of Grandfather's second treatment. While the rain and wind gathered strength, Grandfather seemed to grow weaker. Father said that Grandfather would have to get worse before he could get better. Grandfather had already gotten worse; when was he supposed to get better?

But today the sun shone, and a healthy breeze chased white clouds across a blue sky—perfect kite-flying weather. Hiroshi couldn't wait to show Grandfather the surprise.

The bus lurched to a stop, and the brakes let out a whoosh sigh. Hiroshi didn't even glance in Skye's direction as he got off the bus and raced all the way to his front door.

"I'm home!" He tossed his backpack at the foot of the stairs.

"Shh, Hiro-chan." Mother came down the steps. "Grandfather is resting."

"Can't I wake him up? I have to show him something."

Mother shook her head. "I just gave him his medication a few minutes ago. He should sleep for a couple of hours, at least."

"Hours?" Hiroshi glanced at the hall clock. "It'll be dark by then. I wanted to go to the park."

"Hiroshi, I don't think he's up to it today."

"But when is he supposed to start feeling better?"

Mother frowned. "He's still tired, Hiroshi. Maybe tomorrow." She put her arm around his shoulder. "He just needs some rest."

"But I've got a surprise for him—I repainted the part that Grandfather fixed. The part Skye broke."

"He'll be pleased," Mother said. "You can show him when he wakes up." She glanced out the front window. "It's a beautiful day. Why don't you ask Sorano to fly the kite with you?"

Mother didn't understand anything. There was no way he would ever let Skye touch the dragon kite again. She'd probably ruin it for good.

"I'll just wait for Grandfather—maybe tomorrow."

"You might meet some new friends at the park—lots of children live in our neighborhood."

Our neighborhood. This wasn't Hiroshi's neighborhood. His neighborhood was on the other side of the world.

He carried his backpack upstairs and set it on the desk in his room. He began pulling out his notebooks, then stopped. Maybe Grandfather would still be awake. Hiroshi freed the dragon kite from its hiding place under his bed and inspected the spot he'd painted. Would Grandfather be able to tell where the new *washi* paper joined the old?

Hiroshi stuck his head into the empty hallway. The beeps and clicks from the computer downstairs meant that Mother was in the study, probably emailing one of her sisters. Pausing outside of Grandfather's room, he pressed his ear to the door. Nothing. He knocked—loud enough for Grandfather to hear, but soft enough that Mother wouldn't. When there was no answer, he inched the door open until he could peek into the room.

"Grandfather?" he whispered. Grandfather didn't stir. Hiroshi slipped into the room with the kite, then closed the door behind him. The shades blocked most of the sun, but Hiroshi could still hear the wind rustling through the oak that stood guard outside the window.

He switched on the rice paper lamp and knelt beside the futon. Grandfather had insisted on having a futon when they moved to America. He said he'd never slept in a western bed as long as he'd lived, and he wasn't about to start at the age of eighty-three.

Grandfather wasn't snoring yet, which meant he hadn't been sleeping long. Hiroshi knew Mother would be angry if she found out he woke him up, but Grandfather wouldn't mind. Besides, he'd want to know the kite was all fixed.

"Grandfather?" Hiroshi touched his shoulder. Nothing. "It's me—Hiroshi." He jiggled Grandfather's arm.

Grandfather turned his head and opened one eye. "Hiroshi." He smiled and opened the other eye.

Hiroshi held up the kite. "I have a surprise for you."

Grandfather squinted, looking confused.

"I painted it." He brought the kite closer so Grandfather could see it better. "The fixed part, I mean."

Grandfather brushed his fingertips across the dragon scales Hiroshi had painted. He nodded and smiled. "Well done, Hiroshi. The dragon will be eager to fly again."

Hiroshi jumped up. "I knew you'd want to fly it—I told Mother."

Grandfather's eyes closed. "It is this medicine they give me. I will take a quick nap first. And then we will go." *A quick nap? How long would that be?* Grandfather kept his eyes closed. "Why don't you get your homework done, then come and wake me up?"

123

Hiroshi stood. "Okay." He laid the dragon kite beside the futon. He could tell from Grandfather's breathing that he had fallen asleep once again.

When Hiroshi returned an hour later, snoring came from behind Grandfather's door. He snuck into the room and picked up the kite.

"Grandfather?" He knelt and squeezed his hand. Grandfather snorted once and rolled onto his side. The snoring began again, soft at first, growing louder with each breath.

Hiroshi sighed. He clicked off the lamp and stood, still holding the kite. When he reached the door, he tried one more time. "Grandfather? I'm going now."

More snoring.

Hiroshi closed the door behind him, defeated. He found Mother at the computer. "I'm going to the park." He held the dragon kite in one hand, and the reel in the other.

Mother looked up. "Thank you for letting him sleep."

Hiroshi nodded, then started for the door.

"Hiroshi?"

He stopped, but didn't turn around.

"He'll feel better tomorrow."

Hiroshi shrugged. "That's what you said yesterday."

She put her hand on his shoulder. "I know this is hard. It is difficult for all of us."

Hiroshi nodded. It was all hard—this new place, school, English, and most of all, watching Grandfather get sicker.

Mother smiled. "I have some good news."

"Grandfather doesn't need the treatment anymore?"

Mother smiled a sad smile. "I hope that will be true one day soon."

Hiroshi tried again. "We're all moving back to Japan?"

Mother tilted her head. "Guess again."

Hiroshi sighed.

"I've invited Sorano over tomorrow to begin tutoring. Working around her soccer schedule, we've carved out three days per week for the lessons."

"That's the good news?" Hiroshi raised an eyebrow.

"Now you can start learning English faster and help Sorano prepare for her Japanese exams. What do you think?" She looked like this was the world's best idea.

"Does it have to be three days a week?"

"Four days would be better."

This conversation was not going Hiroshi's way. "Do we have to?"

Mother crossed her arms—which meant yes, they had to.

"I'm going to the park, okay? I'll be back before dinner."

He slammed the door, hurried down the driveway, and headed toward the park. Tutoring sessions with Skye would eat up time he had planned to spend with Grandfather. Maybe if he studied harder, they wouldn't have to tutor each other. But that would mean Skye would have to study harder, too. Not likely.

The wind tugged at the kite, eager to sweep the dragon up into the sky. Hiroshi broke into a jog and didn't stop until he reached the hill overlooking the playground. He stood with his back to the wind and closed his eyes. He took a breath, opened his eyes, and released the kite. It climbed higher and higher, happy to be back in the sky where it belonged.

"It's up! Look at it go!" Hiroshi said before remembering Grandfather wasn't with him. Tomorrow. Tomorrow he'd come back with Grandfather.

He played the line, challenging the dragon to dip and turn and climb even higher. When the kite obeyed, pride welled in Hiroshi's rib cage. But when he thought about Grandfather, doubt and fear settled in—doubt that Grandfather would get better and fear that there wasn't much time left for flying kites together.

21
Skye

Skye spotted Hiroshi as soon as she biked into the park. The dragon was already flapping high over his head. Was he still mad about her stepping on the kite? Just thinking of that sickening crunch of bamboo under her feet made her want to turn around and go home. But there was only one way she could get more time with Grandfather, and that was through Hiroshi the Gatekeeper. *No, more like Hiroshi the Grandfather Keeper.*

Skye stuck her hand in her back pocket to make sure the peace offering was still there, then pedaled around the playground, past the kids playing basketball, and all the way up to the top of the hill. She laid her bike on the grass and walked up behind Hiroshi. He looked hypnotized by the dragon.

That's when Skye noticed the dragon's wound was gone. "Oh! You can't even see where it was."

Hiroshi turned, obviously surprised to see her there. "I painted over that part." He turned back to the kite.

Neither one said a word for a long minute.

Then Skye took a breath. "Look, I'm sorry about the kite." *There. I said it. Again.*

Hiroshi still didn't look at her. "It was an accident."

Skye folded her arms. "So are you accepting my apology or not?"

127

"Yes, I accept your apology." He wound up some of the line without looking her way.

"And that's it?"

"What's it?"

Skye rolled her eyes. She was about to say that it was his turn to apologize for lying when he asked, "Did your parents tell you about the lessons?"

Skye nodded. "My dad said they all think it's this great idea."

"I am not needing help," Hiroshi said, switching to English as if to prove his point.

Skye bit her lip but said nothing.

"What?" He looked mad, like this was her fault.

"Nothing. Here." She pulled the paper from her pocket and thrust it toward him.

"What is it?" Hiroshi looked suspicious.

"It's another English tip."

He eyed the paper.

"It's not poison, you know." Skye kept her hand out. "Here. Take it."

"I do not need English tips."

Oh, yes, you do.

Skye heard the skidding of brakes behind her and turned to see Kevin Donovan getting off his bike. She stepped between Hiroshi and Kevin.

"Hey, cool kite." Kevin looked up.

Is it possible that Kevin could actually be a decent human being?

"So where's the doctor's mask?"

Nope. Not possible.

"Leave him alone, Kevin." Skye took a step toward him. "Just go home."

"Hey, it's a free hill. I can be here."

Hiroshi's voice came from behind her. "What is he saying?"

"You don't want to know."

Kevin raised an eyebrow and opened his mouth, but Skye cut him off before he could say anything.

"Yes, Kevin, I was just speaking in Japanese. Get over it."

Kevin held up his hands like he was innocent.

"And if you don't leave us alone, I'll tell Mrs. Garcia I saw you cheating on the science quiz."

Kevin's face paled. "You wouldn't do that."

"Oh, yes, I would."

"Fine. Hang out with your boyfriend. See if I care." He picked up his bike and coasted down the hill. That had worked out nicely. Skye hadn't even seen Kevin cheating. She'd have to remember that technique next time.

She turned back to Hiroshi. "Trust me. You definitely need the English tips."

"What else was he saying?" Hiroshi asked in Japanese.

"It doesn't matter."

"But I want to know."

"No, you don't. He was being a jerk." Skye handed him the paper. "Just take it."

Hiroshi took the paper from Skye's hand. "I can defend myself, you know."

Skye sighed. "I'm sure you can. But not in English. Not yet."

Hiroshi turned away from her. "I feel like being by myself."

129

Skye had defended him to Kevin Donovan, and now he was acting like she'd insulted him. She couldn't do anything right. "Fine. I have to go to soccer practice anyway." She took off down the hill on her bike, already imagining a Hiroshi-shaped target in the soccer goal.

Hiroshi watched Skye pedal off down the hill. He hated that he needed her to stick up for him.

A tug on his line drew his gaze upward. The dragon's eyes bore down on him, demanding to know where Grandfather was. "He should be here," Hiroshi told the dragon.

Grandfather wasn't supposed to get sick. They weren't supposed to move to America, and he wasn't supposed to be stuck depending on Skye to teach him real English. But he needed English to make friends.

Hiroshi reeled in the line, yanking the dragon lower and lower until he could snatch it from the air. With one last glance down the hill, Hiroshi spotted Ravi on the far side of the playground, facing his direction and waving. But Hiroshi was tired of struggling through English. He pretended not to see Ravi and turned and jogged down the hill toward home.

Hiroshi slammed the door, kicked off his shoes, and stomped up to his room. He let the dragon kite fall to the floor, then remembered the paper in his pocket. He took it out and sank onto his bed. He unfolded the paper and smoothed out the creases. It read:

Skye's English Tip #3
Word of the Day 今日の言葉 : LOSER
Definition: someone who is different and doesn't fit in with the other kids
Example: when you bring an o-bento lunch to school and kids look at your sushi rolls and say, "what's that?" and you tell them it's eel with rice and seaweed, and they say, "Ew! Gross!" you feel like a loser. Even if you're not.

What was gross about sushi? Hiroshi sighed. He'd never figure Americans out.

"Hiroshi?" Father's voice came from the other side of the door. Hiroshi slipped the paper behind him as Father entered the room. "You can't slam doors. Grandfather is—"

"I know—he's sleeping." Hiroshi flopped back onto his bed and stared at the ceiling. "As usual."

Father picked up the kite and set it on Hiroshi's desk. "I know this is hard on you, Hiroshi." The mattress creaked and leaned as Father sat down. Hiroshi rolled over and faced the wall, and Father rested a hand on Hiroshi's shoulder. "We all hope Grandfather will feel better soon."

But Father's voice didn't sound anything like hope. Hiroshi tried to swallow.

"We'll just have to be patient and pray the treatment works." Father patted his shoulder, but Hiroshi shrugged his hand off. Father didn't speak for a full minute. "I'll call you when dinner is ready."

Who cares when dinner is ready? Hiroshi wasn't hungry.

132

The mattress creaked again when Father stood up. Hiroshi heard Father's footsteps pause before he closed the door behind him. Tears burned behind his eyelids, and he squeezed his eyes shut. A few minutes later he heard a soft knock at his door.

"I want to be alone." Still facing the wall, he pulled his pillow over his head.

"May I come in?" Grandfather's voice sounded muffled.

Hiroshi lifted the pillow an inch. "Yes." When Grandfather sat down, the mattress didn't creak; it barely leaned at all.

"What's this?" Grandfather asked.

Hiroshi heard paper crinkle and he rolled over. Grandfather held Skye's paper, but Hiroshi knew he couldn't see the writing without his reading glasses.

"Nothing."

When Grandfather handed the paper to Hiroshi, he balled it up and held it in his fist. "Nothing important."

"I am sorry I slept so long. How was the wind today?"

Hiroshi waited until he was sure his voice would come out steady. "Fine, I guess."

"You told me you painted the new section of the kite—may I see it?"

Hiroshi rolled over and shrugged. "Sure." He lifted the dragon from the desk.

Grandfather pulled his glasses from his shirt pocket. He switched on the nightstand lamp and trained the light on the section where the rip had been.

"Well done, Hiroshi. I cannot tell where my painting stops and yours begins." He nodded. "You have matched the dragon's scales exactly from one side to the other."

133

Hiroshi sat up straighter. "Do you really think so? It took me a long time to do it."

Grandfather smiled. "It is a job well done. We will test it together tomorrow."

"I already tested it." He snuck a glance at Grandfather, then pretended to pick lint off his bedspread.

Grandfather nodded. "Of course." He clicked off the desk lamp. "How did it do?"

"Fine."

Grandfather smiled a tired smile. "I am glad."

Hiroshi sat up. "You were sleeping, you know." He said it like an accusation.

Grandfather nodded again. "We will go to the park tomorrow, if you'd like."

Hiroshi didn't answer right away. He opened his hand far enough to see Skye's paper peeking out. "I don't want to go to the park anymore." He paused. "I want to go back to Japan." Where they had been happy. Where Grandfather wasn't sick. His words became a rogue gust of wind, the kind that threatens to carry kites away against their will. He couldn't stop them from coming.

"I hate it here. I want to go home."

He felt the string snap, felt the greedy wind sweep his kite away. Angry tears streamed down Hiroshi's cheeks, but he didn't try to wipe them away. He hated the cancer. The cancer had forced them to leave Japan. And even after stealing Grandfather's laughter and strength, the cancer still wouldn't leave him alone.

Hiroshi had never spoken to Grandfather with such disrespect. What would Grandfather do? Hiroshi tried breathing slowly, the way Grandfather had taught him to calm his nerves before kite

134

battles. When Hiroshi dared to look, he expected to see anger on Grandfather's face. But he saw only sadness.

The last of the storm inside Hiroshi snuffed itself out. "I'm sorry, Grandfather." The words burned his throat.

Grandfather placed his hand over Hiroshi's. "So am I, Hiroshi. So am I."

Shifting her bulging backpack, Skye lifted the brass knocker on Hiroshi's door. Her shoulders already ached from carrying all those books from her bike to the door. She had seen pictures of Japanese school kids with backpacks like suitcases—and no wheels. She wondered how they did it without tipping over.

The door swung open, and Aunt Naoko welcomed her in with a smile. "It is lovely to see you, Sorano. Thank you for offering to tutor Hiroshi."

Offering? Maybe the word meant something different in Japanese. Or maybe it had a double meaning: *offer = bribe with the promise of the chance to play on the All-Star soccer team.*

"Would you like something to eat or drink? Maybe a warm cup of green tea?"

Green tea? Ugh. But her aunt looked so pleased and sincere that Skye couldn't say no. "*Hai. Domo arigato gozaimasu.* Thank you— green tea sounds . . . great."

Aunt Naoko beamed. "Hiroshi is in the dining room. Please." She swept her arm past the foyer. As Skye headed through the front room, she looked for a plant that might be thirsty for green tea later.

She spotted Hiroshi at the head of the table, scribbling in a notebook. He didn't look up. Books were spread everywhere; the only clear spot was all the way across the table. Skye plopped her books down and sat. Hiroshi didn't stop writing.

Skye sighed. "Look, this wasn't my idea. I don't like this any more than you do."

Hiroshi looked up. "I know."

Aunt Naoko came in with two cups, a pot of green tea, and some kind of pastry on a plate.

"*Arigato, Okaa-san,*" Hiroshi said, and he looked pleased.

"*Arigato gozaimasu,*" Skye said, hoping maybe the pastries were stuffed with some kind of Japanese chocolate.

Aunt Naoko offered the plate to Skye first. "Do you know this pastry?"

"I don't think so." She took one. "Thank you."

Aunt Naoko beamed. "It is called *yomogi mochi.*" She looked at Hiroshi. "I am not sure how you would translate it into English." Skye took a bite as Hiroshi flipped through a Japanese-English dictionary. The pastry was sweet and soft inside. Not bad.

Hiroshi made some notes, then looked up. "It has a bean filling, *tsubushi an,* covered with a layer of sweet rice." Skye looked at the half-eaten pastry in her hand. Her chewing slowed.

"Oh, and *yomogi*—a kind of grass, and roasted soybean on top." Hiroshi looked triumphant. "It is one of my favorites."

Aunt Naoko smiled. "I can give your mother the recipe, if you would like."

Skye commanded her tongue to swallow the bite of pastry, and then she washed it down with a gulp of green tea. "Thank you,

137

Aunt Naoko. It's delicious. But boy, am I full." Skye set the rest of the bean paste–rice–grass concoction on her napkin. "I've got soccer practice later, so I better not fill up too much."

"Of course, Sorano-chan." Aunt Naoko gathered up Hiroshi's mess of books and papers, piling them next to him with a firm look. "*Dozo.* Please, come, Sorano." She pointed to the chair next to Hiroshi. "I apologize for my disorganized son. You will need to sit closer if the two of you are to get any work done." Hiroshi blushed, and Skye slid over one chair.

Aunt Naoko left the room, and Skye unzipped her bag. "So what's first? English or Japanese?" She hoped he'd say English, because she had a new English tip for him. The perfect one, actually. She pulled it out of her notebook.

Hiroshi sighed. "It doesn't matter." He opened a folder and pulled out a piece of paper folded in half. "If you want to start with Japanese, here." He gave her the paper.

Skye frowned. She hadn't even shown him her homework assignment or any of her Japanese books. How did he know what to start with? She eyed the paper, wary.

"Go ahead. It's not a *yomogi mochi,*" he said. She looked up, feeling the heat creep into her cheeks. If Hiroshi had seen right through her polite snack talk, had Aunt Naoko seen, too?

She unfolded the paper and squinted at the Japanese writing. This was too hard—she didn't know all of the characters. "I'm not sure I can read this."

He nodded once. "Try."

She took a breath and began. "*Gomen nasai.*" Okay, that part she knew; it meant "I'm sorry." She scanned the other lines. "Something about Grandfather . . . and the kite?" It was probably something she'd understand if she heard it, but reading all those characters? Forget it.

He took the paper and angled it so Skye could see it. He read it aloud, following the characters down the page with his finger as he spoke in Japanese: "I am sorry that I was not truthful before. I wanted to fly the kite alone with Grandfather. This was not fair to you. I apologize."

Skye felt like she should apologize all over again about stepping on the kite. But she wasn't sorry that she wanted to spend time with Grandfather.

Hiroshi broke into her thoughts. "What's that?"

Skye blinked. "What's what?" She saw his eyes on her English Tip page, and slid it under her notebook. "Oh, it's nothing."

Hiroshi's face fell. "I thought maybe it was a new word. Your kind of word, not a school word."

Skye tapped her pencil on the table. Maybe she shouldn't give him the tip, now that he'd apologized. Would he get mad? She looked at him sideways. It was a word he needed to know.

"Well, I guess I could show you. Since you asked for something new. But it's not about you, or anything."

"Okay." Hiroshi looked doubtful.

She put the paper in front of him. It read:

Ⓐ Skye's English Tip #4
Word of the Day 今日の言葉 : COOL
Definition: when something is awesome, great, or fun
Example: When someone tells you a big, fat lie, that's NOT cool.

139

Hiroshi read the paper, then nodded. "This is about my lie."

Skye shrugged. "I mean, it could be anyone's lie. It's for lies in general, I guess."

Now he looked confused. "How can a lie be fat?"

"Well, it just means *big;* you know, a big lie."

Aunt Naoko's voice came from the next room. "Do either of you need anything?" Skye closed Hiroshi's note of apology and leaned her elbow on it. Hiroshi shoved Skye's English Tip #4 under a notebook just as Aunt Naoko popped her head in the door.

"Do you need more green tea?" She frowned at their closed books.

Skye opened one of Hiroshi's books and said, "We were just doing an English conversation exercise. As soon as we're done, we'll start on Japanese."

Hiroshi nodded.

Aunt Naoko smiled, but it was one of those I've-got-my-eye-on-you smiles. "Let me know if you need anything." Aunt Naoko left and Skye sighed.

"What do you have for homework?" Hiroshi asked. Skye opened to the list of the next set of *kanji* she needed to memorize before Saturday and turned the book so Hiroshi could see it. He inspected the page and nodded. "This will be easy."

"Easy? Maybe for you."

"I will show you—all you need are the right tricks, and you'll know these by Saturday."

Skye raised an eyebrow. "You really think so?"

Hiroshi nodded. "How do you usually study these?"

"Like this." Skye looked at the first *kanji,* then covered it up. "*Isu,*" she said. Then she lifted her hand and checked her answer.

140

"Right, *chair*." She covered up the next one, but before she could say the answer, Hiroshi stopped her.

"That way is not the cool way. It will take forever."

Skye's shoulders slumped. "I know. That's the problem. And I don't have until forever." Skye paused.

Hiroshi turned her book so it was facing her. "You have to find the ones that are related."

"What do you mean?"

Hiroshi pointed to two *kanji* characters. "See? *Tako*, kite, is this one. *Kaze*, wind, is over here. They both begin with the same symbol. Only the centers of each are different."

"Oh!" Skye looked at them as if she were seeing them for the first time. "Why didn't I ever notice that before?"

"You mean your teacher never showed you?"

Skye thought. "You know, maybe she did. I don't always pay attention." Hiroshi nodded, like he knew the feeling.

"You two look like you are working hard." Grandfather's voice came from over Skye's shoulder.

"*Konbanwa*, Grandfather," Skye and Hiroshi said.

Grandfather peered at one of Hiroshi's books. "This must be English."

Skye pointed to her name on her notebook. "English letters are like *hiragana* and *katakana*—there are sounds for each one. Sometimes they have more than one sound, and sometimes you can combine them to make other sounds."

Grandfather nodded. "You are a good teacher, Sorano-chan."

Skye grinned and opened her notebook to a clean page and wrote in large, clear letters. "Here. This says *grandfather* in English."

Grandfather took the notebook and placed his finger on the

141

last letter, *r*. Then he moved his finger to the g and tapped it. "English begins on the left, I've heard."

Skye nodded. "It always goes from left to right." She glanced at Hiroshi, who seemed to be studying some spot on the table in front of him.

Grandfather gave the notebook back to Skye. She tore out the page with Grandfather's name. "You can keep this if you want."

Grandfather smiled. "*Arigato gozaimasu,* Sorano-chan. Perhaps each time you come, I can learn one new word in English. It is never too late to learn something new."

Hiroshi spoke up. "Tomorrow we won't be studying, because Skye has a soccer game."

Grandfather's face brightened. "Why don't we go and cheer her on, Hiroshi?" He turned to Skye. "We've never seen you play, Sorano-chan."

Skye grinned. She might not be brilliant in Japanese or a champion kite flier, but soccer was her chance to show them she was good at something.

Hiroshi frowned. "But I thought we were going to fly the dragon kite tomorrow, Grandfather."

Grandfather nodded. "You are right, Hiroshi. But why don't we go to the game together first? If there is time, we will fly the kite afterward."

Skye grinned again—until she saw that Hiroshi looked miserable.

"Sure," he mumbled. "I'd love to go."

But Skye knew that was a big, fat lie.

Hiroshi hung back, letting the other kids spill out of the bus and in through the front of the school. Skye was at the dentist this morning, so at least he didn't have to worry about running into her for the next few hours. Maybe the dentist would find six cavities, and it would take all day to fill them. And then Skye wouldn't be able to play soccer after school because she'd be home in bed with an ice pack on her jaw. And then he and Grandfather could fly the dragon kite like they'd planned.

The school's front entrance always smelled like pencils and American breakfast. Following the sea of colorful backpacks, Hiroshi strained to pick out familiar words from the voices floating down the hallway. Sometimes he heard languages other than English, but never Japanese.

In the classroom he hung up his jacket, emptied his backpack, and took his seat. He glanced over at Skye's empty desk. It didn't matter that she wasn't in it—he didn't feel like speaking to her anyway, in Japanese or in English.

Surrounded by his classmates' conversations and laughter, Hiroshi found he could understand more of their words now. But speaking was still a problem. What if he made a mistake? What if no one could understand him? Mr. Jacobs hadn't given Hiroshi any more baby books after listening to him read last week. Now

Hiroshi was reading chapter books, but they still weren't as long as the other fifth graders' books. He'd just have to study more.

As soon as the bell rang, Hiroshi rushed through the math warm-up, willing the clock to jump ahead a half hour. When nine o'clock finally came, he rushed to ESL class—the only place where he could speak in English without worrying about sounding completely stupid.

"I saw your kite," Ravi said. "The other day, at the park."

"You did?" Hiroshi pretended this was news, hoping Ravi hadn't realized that he'd seen him, too.

Ravi nodded. "But then you run away. Fast." He smiled. "We fly kites in India, too. Next time, I can fly it?"

Hiroshi smiled. "Yes. Okay—next time." It could be fun to show the dragon to someone who already knew about kites—one afternoon when Grandfather was resting, maybe.

Mr. Jacobs slid a piece of paper in front of Hiroshi. "Hiroshi, I have a surprise for you today." Hiroshi glanced at the paper. English words and Japanese characters surrounded a picture of a kite. Hiroshi's eyes drank in the Japanese words:

National Cherry Blossom Festival
in Washington, DC March 25–April 9
Featuring the Annual National Cherry Blossom Kite Festival
Sunday, April 9, from 10 a.m. to 4 p.m.
on the National Mall
Come and see handmade kites, kite stunts, and the *rokkaku* kite battle!

144

Could it be true? A kite battle in America? He looked up to find Mr. Jacobs grinning.

"The Cherry Blossom Festival is held each year by the Japan-America Society of Washington, DC," Mr. Jacobs said. "They've got Japanese crafts, food, music—it's lots of fun."

"It says a kite battle," Hiroshi said.

"Oh, yes—they have kites. And the kite battle is the best part. It's on the last day of the festival." Mr. Jacobs clapped once and rubbed his hands together. "You would love it, and so would your grandfather, I'll bet."

"Thank you." Hiroshi grinned. He folded up the flyer and stuffed it in his pocket. He couldn't wait to see Grandfather's face when he told him the good news.

Hiroshi threw open the front door of his house, waving the flyer back and forth.

"Grandfather!"

"Son?" Father's voice called from the kitchen.

Hiroshi ran into the kitchen, stopping to catch his breath. "Where's Grandfather? There's something I have to show him."

Father's tie was loose, and his shirt was wrinkled. And he was home when he should have been at work.

"Have a seat, Hiroshi." It was never good news when Hiroshi's father told him to have a seat. Anyway, he didn't feel like sitting— he had to find Grandfather right away.

His father pulled out a chair. Hiroshi sat.

"What is it?"

Father folded and unfolded his hands. "Hiroshi, we need to talk about Grandfather."

Father must have found out how disrespectful I was to Grandfather when I said I hated it here. Hiroshi looked at his shoes. "I didn't mean to say those things."

"What things?" Father looked confused. So Grandfather hadn't told, after all.

"What did you want to tell me?"

Father paused. "We met with his doctors today." Hiroshi's mouth went dry. Father ran his hand through his hair. "They're not going to continue the treatment, Hiroshi."

Hiroshi stood. "But why? They barely started."

Father closed his eyes. He took a breath before opening them again. "The cancer has spread. It's too late."

Hiroshi didn't move. A cold wind burned through him. He glanced at the flyer clenched in his fist and felt a glimmer of hope pushing the cold wind back until it sputtered and died. Hiroshi unfurled his fingers from the paper, smoothed it, folded it up, and slipped it into his jacket pocket.

Grandfather wouldn't want to miss the battle. Maybe it would give him hope. It wasn't too late to hope.

The ride to the hospital seemed to take forever. A part of Hiroshi wished they could drive faster; another part didn't want the ride to end. A hundred questions ran through his head.

"Does cancer hurt?"

Father kept his eyes on the road. When he spoke his voice sounded raw. "He's in some pain, but it comes and goes. They've

146

given him some medication, so I don't know if he'll be awake when we get there or not."

It seemed all Grandfather ever did these days was sleep. "Isn't there some other kind of medicine he can take?"

Hiroshi's father shook his head. "I'm afraid not, Son." The hum of the car's motor was too loud. Outside, an angry wind whipped tree branches back and forth, sending roadside litter swirling into the air. Hiroshi knew how the wind felt.

When they arrived at the hospital, Mother was standing outside Grandfather's room, a crumpled tissue in her hand, her eyes puffy and red. "You go ahead, Hiroshi. He's asked for you several times now."

Hiroshi pushed open the door and stepped into the room. The only light came from a lamp above the headboard—thin, watery light that added wrinkles and shadows to Grandfather's face. His eyes were closed, so Hiroshi sat on the edge of a chair next to the bed and waited. His fingers found the flyer in his pocket. He took it out and started to unfold it.

"What have you got there?"

"Grandfather, you're awake," Hiroshi whispered. He jumped up and stood by the bed.

"You don't have to whisper—there's nothing wrong with my ears, you know." Grandfather smiled and patted Hiroshi's hand. "Those fancy doctors are letting me go home in a few days. What's that you've got there?"

"There's a *rokkaku* battle in a few weeks, in Washington, DC. Can we enter?"

"All that worrying about missing the battle back in Japan." Grandfather chuckled. "Just shows that worrying does no good."

147

Grandfather still hadn't answered the question. Hiroshi swallowed. "We can enter with the dragon kite if you want. Now that it's fixed and everything."

Grandfather smiled. "It's as good as new." Hiroshi knew the kite would never be as good as new, and he suspected Grandfather knew it, too.

"Don't worry about the battle, Grandfather. I'll do the flying, and you'll be next to me, doing the telling." Hiroshi searched for hope on Grandfather's face. Because if Grandfather had hope, Hiroshi could have some, too.

Grandfather smiled—a brave smile, not a hopeful one. He squeezed Hiroshi's hand. "Promise me you'll enter, even if I'm not by your side to do the telling."

"Sure you'll be there, Grandfather. We'll win this one together." Hiroshi knew his words didn't sound brave.

Grandfather patted his hand. "Promise me, just in case."

Hiroshi looked down at Grandfather's wrinkled hand. "I promise," he whispered.

But Grandfather's heavy breathing told Hiroshi he had already fallen asleep.

Skye

"Skye! Heads up!" Coach Tess yelled—and a ball whizzed past Skye's ear.

Skye sprinted downfield after the ball until the referee's final whistle mercifully ended the game—and her misery. She bent over, hands on her knees, and closed her eyes. She'd been off her game, missing four goal shots that should've been cake. Every time she'd messed up, she'd looked at the sidelines to see if Grandfather had made it to the game yet. Where was he? Maybe it was better that he hadn't showed—now he could still think of her as a star soccer player.

As Coach Tess was rehashing the game in the team huddle, Skye glanced at the sidelines and saw her mom was finally off her cell phone. She never took calls during games, and Skye wondered what had been so important. Was it about Grandfather? Maybe he was feeling tired again. Maybe Hiroshi had lied and convinced Grandfather that Skye had been kicked off the team. Considering the way she'd played today, she wouldn't be surprised if that happened.

"Skye!" Her mom was waving her over as the teams finished their high fives down center field.

"Hey, Mom. Where's Grandfather?"

Her mom reached for Skye's soccer bag. "We need to get going, sweetheart."

As they threaded through the maze of coolers, bags, and soccer parents in folding canvas chairs, Skye felt a knot growing in her gut. "Where's Grandfather?"

Her mom didn't break her stride. "We'll talk in the car."

Usually Skye liked to hang around with the team and Coach Tess after the games, analyzing every play. But today she couldn't wait to leave. When they finally reached the car, Skye let her questions fly. "Mom, what's wrong? Something's wrong, isn't it? Is it Grandfather?"

Skye's mom put the key in the ignition but didn't start the car. Her hand fell onto her lap, and she picked at the outside seam of her jeans. Then she turned to Skye, tears brimming in her eyes. "Yes, Skye. It's Grandfather."

Skye stood outside the hospital door. Through the sliver of a window, she could see Hiroshi sitting by Grandfather's bed. Hiroshi's back was facing the door, so Skye knew he hadn't seen her yet. Grandfather was sleeping.

"I don't know if I can go in."

"Of course you can." Skye's dad rested his hand on her shoulder. "He was asking about you earlier." Skye nodded, but her feet stayed glued to the floor. Grandfather looked small in the hospital bed with all the buttons and levers. His skin was pale next to the sky-blue gown. "You can wait until he's awake, if you'd like," her dad said softly.

Skye stared through the window at Hiroshi's back. He was

slumped in his chair, folding and unfolding a piece of paper. None of this was fair. How could she get to know Grandfather better if he was sick all the time? "I'm going in."

Hiroshi must not have heard her, because he jumped when she pulled up a chair next to his. He folded the paper and slipped it into his pocket. They sat for a while in silence, shoulder to shoulder, watching Grandfather.

"How is he?" Skye whispered.

Hiroshi shrugged. "They do not tell me so much."

Grandfather stirred, then opened his eyes. "Is that English you two are speaking? I'll have to start learning to keep up with the both of you." He smiled.

"Grandfather!" Skye jumped up, and Hiroshi joined her. She wanted to take Grandfather's hand but was unsure with Hiroshi there. She still felt like she was intruding. "How are you feeling?"

He chuckled. "Much better, thank you." He waved at the tubes and machines around him. "They go to so much fuss. I think it makes the doctors feel better." Skye nodded—but she knew all of this stuff wasn't there to make the doctors feel better. "How was your soccer game? I am sorry I missed it."

"It was . . ." Skye winced, thinking of how she'd played. "It was not so great. Good thing you didn't have to sit through that."

Grandfather smiled and patted her hand. "Next time will be better."

Skye hoped her smile looked more cheerful than she felt. "Thank you, Grandfather. I hope so."

"Did Hiroshi tell you the news?" Grandfather asked.

"News?" Skye looked at Hiroshi, but he looked confused, too.

"Yes, yes. About the kite festival."

Hiroshi looked at the floor, hands shoved in his pockets.

"What kite festival?"

"There will be a *rokkaku* kite battle in Washington, DC. Why don't you show her the flyer, Hiroshi?"

Showing her the flyer was probably the last thing Hiroshi wanted to do. It took him ages to pull it out of his pocket—that must be the paper he'd been holding earlier. He passed it to Skye and she unfolded it. The National Cherry Blossom Kite Festival—with a *rokkaku* kite battle.

"I'll come and watch you." She handed the paper back to Hiroshi, who actually looked grateful.

Grandfather smiled at Hiroshi. "We have been practicing for this moment for many years. Hiroshi is ready to fly the kite on his own." He turned to Skye. "But he will need someone to hold the reel and keep track of the line. It is a very important role."

"But Grandfather, you—" Hiroshi began.

"Should be the one to do that," Skye finished.

Grandfather's smile looked sad. "It is time for someone else to take a turn." He patted Skye's hand. "Sorano, will you take my place at Hiroshi's side during the kite battle?"

"Grandfather, you can still be in the kite battle," Hiroshi said, his voice pleading.

Skye agreed. "You can do it, Grandfather. I'll come and watch and cheer you both on."

"Right," Hiroshi said. "Skye—Sorano—can come and learn and we'll show her what to do and she can try it next time, and—"

Skye was already nodding. "I'll take careful notes, and then—"

Grandfather closed his eyes, and both Skye and Hiroshi fell silent. Waiting. Was he asleep again? He smiled before he opened

152

his eyes again. "I won't discuss it any longer. You are both ready. I ask for your promise."

Skye and Hiroshi looked at each other then back at Grandfather.

"*Yakusoku*," they said.

Of all the Japanese words Skye had learned since she met Grandfather, "promise" was the hardest to say.

Hiroshi sat on the front porch step, waiting. Father had called to say that he and Grandfather were on their way home, but that was a half hour ago. Where were they? Mother and First Uncle came out onto the porch.

First Uncle had dropped Skye off at Japanese school this morning. At least she wouldn't be around if Grandfather felt well enough to fly the dragon. Mother had said that Grandfather might be tired when he first got home. But Hiroshi knew the dragon and the wind were like medicine to Grandfather. Hiroshi couldn't let go of hope.

Finally a car pulled up to the house, followed by a truck—but Hiroshi didn't recognize either one. He felt Mother's hand on his shoulder.

"This is the woman we told you about." Father had told him that a lady would show them how to make Grandfather more comfortable at home. Hiroshi already knew how to do that: take him back to Japan.

Two big men got out of the truck, circled around to the back end, and yanked open the doors. A tall lady stepped out of the car, carrying a briefcase. Hiroshi, Mother, and First Uncle watched in silence as the lady clicked up the front walk in her high heels.

"Good morning, Mr. and Mrs. Tsuki." The lady smiled and tucked her hair behind one ear. She'd pronounced their last name the American way, with a t-sound: *tuh-SOO-kee*. She should have said *tzoo-kee*, of course. No one corrected her.

"Please, come in," Mother said.

The lady walked in, her quick eyes sweeping over the front room, and then she turned. She smiled at Hiroshi. "I'm Fran Grimley. It's nice to meet you. . . ."

"Hiroshi." He held out his hand, remembering that Americans didn't bow. Mother cleared her throat and he remembered to add, "Hello, Mrs. Fran."

Hiroshi knew right away that he'd made a mistake. Too late, he remembered that Americans say their given name first, like that was more important than their family name. "I mean, Mrs. Grimley."

She gave him a warm smile. "You can call me either one." Hiroshi nodded, wishing Father would hurry up and get here with Grandfather.

"Well, then." Mrs. Grimley turned back to Mother and First Uncle. "I know you've been told how the hospice program works, but I'm glad to answer any questions you may have." Hiroshi frowned. *Hospice* sounded a lot like *hospital.*

Mrs. Grimley stepped into the front room. "We'll have the bed set up in no time, and I'll show you how it works." Her eyes ran to the top of the stairs. "We recommend the bed be set up downstairs. Would you like it here, in the living room?"

Hiroshi knew they were bringing a special bed for Grandfather. But in the living room? Maybe Hiroshi had misunderstood.

First Uncle nodded. "Yes, that will be fine."

155

"Grandfather doesn't like beds," Hiroshi said. "He says his futon is fine for him."

Mother turned to him. "Hiroshi, why don't you go and ride your bike?" He expected her to scold him for being rude, but her eyes were sad. "You can watch for Father and Grandfather. They should be here soon."

That was fine with him. Hiroshi didn't want to miss the moment when Grandfather found out about the living-room bed. He'd send it back, for sure. Hiroshi swung open the door, and then stopped. One of the men from the truck had his stubby thumb poised to ring the doorbell.

"Hello there, Son."

Hiroshi pointed to the bed. "We do not need that. Thank you." Too bad they had unloaded it for nothing.

"Hiroshi." He heard the warning in Mother's voice. "Your bike?" She nodded towards the garage.

He brushed past the men, leaving them and their bed behind. As soon as he stepped around them, he saw Father getting out of the car.

"Grandfather, you're home!" Hiroshi ran to Grandfather's door and yanked it open.

Grandfather leaned out and peered at the sky. "It is a good day for flying, isn't it?"

Father shut the trunk. "Hiroshi, would you give me a hand?"

"Sure—" He took a step toward Father, then stopped. "What's that?" He didn't know why he'd asked, because he already knew.

Father unfolded the wheelchair with a snap. Hiroshi stared, not wanting to touch it. He barely noticed when Father came around to help Grandfather out of the car.

"How do you like my new wheels?" Grandfather nodded in the direction of the chair. In Hiroshi's mind, he could see Grandfather running next to him through the village streets—back in Japan, laughing and racing like kites on the wind. How could this be the same Grandfather?

"Hiroshi?" Father pointed his chin toward the chair. Hiroshi pushed the chair over to where Grandfather stood. Father had one hand under Grandfather's arm and the other around his waist. He lowered Grandfather into the chair as if he were made of glass. Grandfather was breathing fast, like he'd been chasing kites all morning.

Hiroshi pushed the chair up the walk, then came to a stop at the front step.

"We'll need to get a ramp," Father said.

"I can help you lift him—it's only one step."

Father shook his head. "It's too heavy."

"No, it's not—I can do it." Hiroshi knelt on one knee and gripped the handlebars from up underneath, his elbows pointing toward the ground. "Okay, I'm ready. You get the front end."

"No, Hiroshi—it's too heavy. Grandfather could fall. Let me ask the men who delivered the bed. They must be inside."

"I can do it!" Hiroshi said. "I won't let him fall."

"Enough." Grandfather's eyes flashed. He placed one hand on either arm of the chair, and scooted himself forward until he perched on the edge of the seat. "You do not need to talk as if I weren't here. I can do it myself."

The breeze paused, holding its breath.

Grandfather's arms trembled as he began to lift himself.

Father stepped forward. "Here—let me—"

157

"I said I can do it." Grandfather's voice held the promise of anger, like gathering winds before a storm. Beads of sweat appeared on his forehead. Hiroshi wished he could command the wind to lift Grandfather to his feet. But the breeze just tiptoed away like a coward.

Grandfather finally stood up—not straight, but at least he was up. When he looked at Hiroshi, his face relaxed into a real smile. "Not bad for an old man!" He rested a shaky foot on the step. "I might need a hand. Just this once." His voice was soft again.

Hiroshi held out his arm, and Grandfather leaned on him. He no longer towered over Hiroshi—had Hiroshi grown, or was Grandfather shrinking?

"We're home!" Father called, opening the front door.

Hiroshi leaned in close to Grandfather's ear. "Some men brought a bed for you." He waited for Grandfather to protest.

"I know. They told me at the hospital." Grandfather nodded and patted Hiroshi's arm.

Hiroshi frowned. *Grandfather already knows? Why isn't he angry?*

Mrs. Grimley and her shoes tapped into the room, followed by Mother and First Uncle. Mrs. Grimley held out her hand to Grandfather, but he didn't take it. He bowed—no, more like a quick nod—and frowned. Now Grandfather would tell the lady he didn't want the bed. Hiroshi bit the inside of his cheek so he wouldn't smile.

Mother translated the part about the bed to Grandfather.

"Thank you." Grandfather nodded again.

Thank you? Is that all he has to say?

"You're welcome." Mrs. Grimley looked as if sleeping in a

158

hospital bed right there in the living room were perfectly normal.

"I've explained everything to your son and daughter-in-law, sir, but I'd be happy to show you how it all works."

Father translated her words to Grandfather, who put his hand on Hiroshi's shoulder. "Please tell her that I thank her for her time. But I have an appointment with my grandson. Now, if you all will excuse us, we'll be on our way." He turned to Hiroshi. "Why don't you run up and get the dragon kite?"

Hiroshi sprinted up to his room, taking three steps at a time— he didn't want to give Grandfather time to change his mind. When he flew back down the stairs with the kite in his hand, the adults all stopped talking at the same time. Mrs. Grimley wasn't smiling anymore, and neither was Mother. First Uncle looked like he'd just swallowed the words he wanted to say, and Father's eyes pleaded with Grandfather.

Grandfather smiled at Hiroshi. "Shall we?" Hiroshi held out his arm for Grandfather, and together they stepped outside, where the wheelchair was waiting.

"We'd better take the chair," Grandfather said. Hiroshi's heart sank. First the bed, now the chair. Grandfather lowered himself into the wheelchair, and Hiroshi handed him the dragon kite. "They'd never forgive me if I refused the chair, too." He looked back at the window, where Hiroshi's parents and First Uncle stood with Mrs. Grimley. Grandfather smiled at them and waved. They waved back but didn't smile.

"Especially since I told them I won't be sleeping in that bed."

Hiroshi started pushing the chair down the driveway. "You really told them that? I knew you'd send the bed back!"

Grandfather chuckled. "Oh, I didn't send it back. I told them they could put it anywhere they wanted to. But I won't be sleeping in it." Hiroshi laughed. "Bad for my health—I'd fall out and break something for sure." Grandfather smacked the arm of the chair twice. "Doesn't this thing go any faster?"

Hiroshi grinned and broke into a jog. "Hang on!" The wind tugged at the edges of the kite, but Grandfather held it down. He leaned his head back and closed his eyes. Hiroshi slowed, then leaned forward to look at Grandfather. "Are you okay, Grandfather?"

He opened one eye and smiled at Hiroshi. "I'm wondering what it would be like to be a kite—to be carried by the wind."

"I'll show you." Hiroshi began jogging again, faster this time. He laughed along with Grandfather, wishing the wind could lift them both into the air.

When the park came into view, Hiroshi hesitated before crossing the street. Although he knew Skye was at Japanese school today, he still half expected her to be there on the hill. But other than two boys playing basketball, there was no one else around.

"It looks like we've got the hill all to ourselves," Grandfather said, smiling.

"Right." Hiroshi usually cut straight up the hill over the grass, but he knew he couldn't make it with Grandfather's wheelchair. Instead, he followed the longer path that gently wound to the top.

Grandfather handed him the kite. "The wind is strong enough for a solo launch." Grandfather was right; Hiroshi got the kite into the air on his first try.

"Nicely done, Hiroshi!" Although Hiroshi had his eyes on the dragon kite, he could hear the smile in Grandfather's voice.

"It looks good, doesn't it, Grandfather?"

"It is flying well today." Hiroshi looked back at Grandfather—and had to look down. He'd forgotten Grandfather was not standing, but sitting in the wheelchair.

"Hiroshi!" He turned to see Ravi running up the path.

"Hi, Ravi."

"You are back! I see your kite from my window." Ravi pointed to a beige house with dark-green shutters across the street. Then he looked up at the dragon. "Is a beautiful kite."

Grandfather cleared his throat.

"Ravi, this is my grandfather." Then he switched to Japanese: "Grandfather, this is my friend Ravi. He's in my English class at school. He used to fly kites, too, in India."

"Hello, sir." Ravi pressed the palms of his hands together and dipped his chin.

Grandfather smiled and nodded. "Ravi, it is nice to meet you."

Ravi gazed up at the kite. "May I try?"

Hiroshi hesitated and glanced at Grandfather.

"Go ahead, Hiroshi," Grandfather said. "You can show him what he needs to do."

Hiroshi handed the reel to Ravi, who beamed.

"Thank you." Ravi squinted into the sun, then looked at Hiroshi like he was trying to think of the right words. "Is been a long time, but I think I remember how to fly." The dragon began a lazy fall, as if sensing that less-skilled hands were now in control. Ravi reeled in the line until it was taut, but the dragon continued to drop.

"Give more line." Hiroshi kept his eyes on the kite.

161

"More?" Ravi sounded unsure.

"Yes, the kite will go up. You will see." Ravi let the line go slack, and sure enough, the kite found a gust of wind and began to rise.

Hiroshi remembered what Grandfather always said: "You can't force a kite to obey. Sometimes you must trust it to find its way."

Hiroshi tried to think of the words in English. "Sometimes you let the kite fly by himself. He knows how to fly." Ravi nodded and grinned.

"Ravi!" The wind carried a boy's voice up the hill from the basketball court.

Ravi waved, then pointed to the dragon. "Hey! Look at the kite!"

The boy cupped his hands around his mouth. "Do you guys want to play?"

Ravi turned to Hiroshi. "You play basketball?"

Hiroshi nodded, although it had been a while. "Yes—" he began. He glanced at Grandfather, then turned to Ravi. "But I must practice for the kite battle. It is in two weeks."

"You go ahead, Hiroshi," Grandfather said. "I will remain here with the kite."

"It's okay, Grandfather. I would rather fly the kite with you." He turned to Ravi and switched back to English. "I am sorry for this time, but I will play another day. Okay?"

Ravi looked disappointed, but said, "Yes, another time." He waved and jogged down the hill to join the other boys.

Grandfather and Hiroshi were silent for a few minutes, their eyes on the kite. "Go with your friend, Hiroshi. The kite is flying itself. I'll be able to watch your game from here."

"I won't leave you alone, Grandfather."

Grandfather winked. "Don't you think it's time I had a turn with the dragon?"

Hiroshi looked at Grandfather. "Of course." He handed over the reel. "I'll just stay and watch."

"It is time you made some friends your age, Hiroshi. Besides Sorano, of course." Hiroshi looked sideways at Grandfather. Did he suspect that Sorano was the last person he wanted for a friend?

"Go on," Grandfather said gently. "It would give me great pleasure to meet your friends after the game."

There was no way Hiroshi could get out of this without being rude to Grandfather. He looked toward the basketball court. "I'll just play for five minutes, and then I'll come back."

"Take your time." Grandfather was already watching the dragon soar above their heads.

Hiroshi sped down the hill. When he reached the court, he recognized one of the boys from his class.

"Hey, you're the new kid, aren't you?" the boy said, tossing the ball from one hand to the other.

Hiroshi nodded. "My name is Hiroshi."

"I'm Carlos."

Ravi pointed to the other boy. "And this is Bilal."

"Okay, we'll play two-on-two," Carlos said, spinning the ball on his finger. "Me and Ravi against Hiroshi and Bilal." Hiroshi hoped American basketball had the same rules as Japanese basketball.

Carlos tossed the ball to Ravi, who started dribbling toward the basket. Hiroshi blocked Ravi, and Bilal stole the ball, then took a shot before Carlos could reach him.

"Two points!" Bilal punched his fist into the air.

163

Now Ravi dribbled the ball onto the court. He paused, pumping the ball before nodding to Carlos. Hiroshi rushed up to Ravi and reached one arm to the left. When Ravi dodged to the right, Hiroshi was ready; he scooped the ball away from Ravi and lobbed it toward Bilal, who was waiting under the basket. Bilal leaped and hooked the ball into the basket.

"Yes!" Bilal grinned at Hiroshi. "Hey—nice pass!"

Hiroshi's heart kept time with his breathing. Had Grandfather seen him? He glanced back at the top of the hill, and his stomach dropped. Grandfather sat motionless, his chin resting on his chest.

"Grandfather!" He never should have left him alone. Hiroshi raced to the top of the hill.

When Hiroshi touched his arm, Grandfather raised his head and opened his eyes. "What—Hiroshi?" He yawned.

"Are you all right?"

"I must have nodded off."

Hiroshi hadn't realized he had been holding his breath until it came rushing out. Grandfather had been asleep. That was all—everything was fine.

Ravi ran up behind him. "He is okay?"

Grandfather held up his empty hands, then stiffened. "The kite—where did it go?"

"Tsuki-san?"

Skye's head snapped up just in time to see Kumamoto Sensei mark something in her grade book—another not-paying-attention mark, no doubt. Skye wondered how many marks were next to her name now—at least one for every line on her teacher's pursed lips.

"*Hai,* Kumamoto Sensei." Skye bowed her head. "*Gomen nasai.*" There may have been lots of Japanese words Skye didn't know, but *I'm sorry* was the one thing she had down.

Next Saturday would be the final exams, but all Skye could think about was Grandfather. While Kumamoto Sensei scanned the page for another verb to shoot her way, Skye glanced at the clock. Ten thirty. Grandfather was supposed to be home from the hospital by now.

"To wear." Kumamoto Sensei nodded. "Use the verb in first person, present tense." Kumamoto Sensei held up a card showing a hat.

Skye swallowed. She'd studied this list with Hiroshi and knew that *kaburu* was for putting something on your head. "*Boushi o kaburu?*"

Kumamoto Sensei peered at Skye over her glasses. "Is that a question or your answer?"

Maya the Wonder Student looked at Skye like she wanted to give her the answer. But this time Skye already knew the answer.

"*Hai, boushi o kaburu,*" Skye said, leaving off the question mark. Kumamoto Sensei nodded, then flipped to a card showing a pair of eyeglasses. *Breathe in,* Skye reminded herself. You know this one. *It's "hang" instead of "wear."*

"*Megane o kakeru.*" Skye's voice was loud and clear.

"Correct." But Kumamoto Sensei didn't smile until Skye had successfully announced that she wore pants, shoes, a shirt, a scarf, a watch, and gloves.

"One more." Kumamoto Sensei flipped over the last card that showed a pair of earrings.

Skye's smile faded. The Japanese word for earrings sounded a lot like the English word: *iyaringu.* It was the "I wear" part that stumped her. Her ears weren't pierced, so she'd never uttered that phrase before. She certainly had never heard her dad say it, and her mom only ever said it in English.

Skye touched her earlobe, as if that would help. It didn't. Some earrings were the hanging kind, so maybe it was the same verb she used for glasses. That must be it. She took a breath. "*Iyaringu o kakeru.*"

Some of the other students giggled, but Kumamoto Sensei hushed them with a glare. "The phrase you are looking for is *Iyaringu o tsukeru.* Please add that to your study guide for next week."

"*Hai,* Kumamoto-sensei." Skye sank into her seat. *Tsukeru . . . tsukeru . . .* what did that mean?

Maya the Walking Dictionary turned and whispered, "*Tsukeru* means *to insert* or *to put on.*"

166

"Thanks," Skye whispered, miserable. Why did one little error make her feel like she'd already flunked next week's exams? Skye barely listened as the others conjugated verbs without a single mistake. Of course.

But how many of them could fly kites? Not that Skye was as good as Hiroshi or Grandfather, but she was learning. She looked out the window, half hoping to see the dragon kite up there with the clouds. But that was impossible, since she was miles away from the park.

When the clock finally struck eleven, Kumamoto Sensei announced that since it was such a nice day, the students could take their break outside. Skye wished she could just stay in and eat alone.

"Tsuki-san, may I please speak with you?" The other kids looked relieved their names hadn't been called as they filed out the door with their *o-bento* boxes.

"*Hai,* Sensei?" Skye hoped this wouldn't take long. No doubt she was in trouble for not studying enough or not paying attention enough. For not being Japanese enough.

As she approached her teacher's desk, she tried to read Kumamoto Sensei's expression. Skye always knew when Mrs. Garcia was mad or proud or tired. But Kumamoto Sensei's face gave away nothing. She removed her glasses and Skye looked at the floor.

"Tsuki-san, you have improved tremendously in recent weeks. I applaud your efforts."

Skye looked up cautiously, wondering if Kumamoto Sensei was joking. But her teacher's eyes looked sincere. "Thank you." Skye smiled. "I will be ready for the exams next week, Kumamoto Sensei."

Her teacher nodded. "Use your time wisely this week, Tsuki-san.

You must pass each exam with an almost perfect score in order to move into the advanced class for the next term."

Almost perfect? Skye's smile faded. Scaling Mount Fuji would have been easier than getting almost perfect exam scores.

"Your conversational skills are excellent, but you must pay close attention—especially in grammar and writing." Her usual stony glare had disappeared, replaced by sympathy that somehow made Skye feel worse. Kumamoto Sensei leaned against her desk and clasped her hands in front of her. "I see great potential in you."

"In me?" Skye looked behind her. Maybe Maya the Perfect had crept back into the room.

"Yes, in you."

"But . . . but I am the worst one in the class."

"You are the only one of my students who was not raised in Japan, Tsuki-san. It is natural to be less familiar with vocabulary and rules of grammar."

Skye would never have guessed that her teacher actually thought she might be good at Japanese. "I will study hard this week, Sensei."

Kumamoto Sensei nodded before returning to the chair behind her desk. Skye retrieved her *o-bento* box and headed for the door.

"Tsuki-san," her teacher called.

Skye paused at the door. "*Hai?*"

"Do not study hard this week."

What? Skye's shoulders sagged. Kumamoto Sensei must have thought there was no use in even trying to pass. Or at least with almost perfect scores.

"The exams are important, and of course you must study. But not only this week." Kumamoto Sensei's voice seemed to echo in

168

the empty classroom. "Become a lifelong learner of your language."

My language? Skye looked at her teacher, who had already gone back to grading papers. "Hai, Sensei," Skye said, and slipped out the door to join her class.

She popped off the lid of her *o-bento* box and slid the chopsticks from their case. Now that her dad had rediscovered his Japanese cooking side, her food looked like all the others'. Skye listened to the perfect Japanese all around her. Sure, her grammar had improved, thanks to Hiroshi. And if she ever went to Japan, maybe she could pass as a native speaker in the first few words of a conversation. But if she had to talk about anything too complicated, she'd be sunk.

She never felt like a tongue-tied imposter when she spoke with Grandfather, though. He always seemed to see straight into the heart of whatever she was trying to say. Skye wanted to show Grandfather that she was good at Japanese, that it mattered to her. That he mattered to her.

She snuck a glance at Maya the Chopstick Expert, who was sitting next to her, chatting with the others in between bites. This was Skye's chance to practice. To get better. Maybe learn a word or two that she could use during the kite-flying lessons.

Skye took a breath. "What did your mom pack in your box today?" she asked. *What a stupid question,* Skye chided herself. Everyone's *o-bento* box was open—it's not like the contents were a secret or anything.

Maya paused, her chopsticks poised midair, looking as if Skye had just spoken in Arabic. Maybe Skye should have kept her big mouth shut and left Japanese to the Japanese kids. Maya swallowed her bite of sushi and washed it down with cold green tea. Then she grimaced and leaned toward Skye. In a hushed voice

169

she said, "If I have to eat any more of my mother's sushi rolls, I think I'll throw up."

Skye's dumpling slipped from her chopsticks and plopped back into the *o-bento* box. She turned to Maya. "Really? I thought you liked them. I do."

Maya shrugged. "They're okay. But my mom never makes anything American." Maya looked up and down the table, then lowered her voice again. "The problem is, no one here has anything good to trade. Like a bologna sandwich with mayo and lettuce."

Skye laughed. "Maya the Bologna-Sandwich Eater. I never would have guessed."

Maya's eyes opened wide and she grinned. "I love bologna. But my mom doesn't."

Skye chewed on a dumpling and thought about what Maya had said. She liked most of the stuff her dad made, but not all of it. She didn't like all of her mom's recipes, either—especially meat loaf.

"I'll tell you what," Skye said. "Next Saturday I'll bring you a bologna sandwich. Mayo and lettuce, right?"

Maya smiled. "And I'll bring you one of my mom's *eho-maki*. I'll need some good-fortune rolls for my exam."

Skye doubted Maya needed any luck. "Just in case," Skye added, "I'll use the lucky bologna for our sandwiches." Maya laughed.

Skye realized that they'd been speaking in Japanese the whole time, and she hadn't even thought of grammar once. She hadn't needed to search her brain for a single Japanese word. In soccer, every move came naturally to Skye. With Japanese, nothing felt natural. Until now. Maybe her Japanese wasn't perfect, but it felt like it was becoming a part of her—a part that she'd never realized was missing.

Hiroshi scanned the skies for the runaway dragon. This was all his fault. If anything happened to the dragon, it would take forever to make another one. And Grandfather didn't have forever.

"There!" Ravi pointed. The dragon was making its way toward a grove of pine trees at the edge of the park, dragging the line and the reel behind it.

"I'll get it!" Hiroshi sprinted down the hill, gaining momentum and pumping his legs until they burned. He had to get that kite.

When he caught up with the reel, it skittered and bounced along the ground just ahead of him. He tried to bend over and catch it, but the kite teased him, keeping the reel just out of his reach. The only way he could stop it now was to step on the line that slithered through the grass. He leaped—one leg stretched in front and the other trailing behind. He pounced, then felt the line grow taut under his sneaker as the runaway kite was jerked back.

"I've got you!" Hiroshi grabbed the reel. But when he turned his attention skyward, his eyes grew wide. "No!"

The dragon had flipped upside down and was diving fast—too fast. Hiroshi let out some line, willing the kite to climb back up. It found a pillow of wind, wobbled, and then righted itself. But it still hung too low, hovering above the road—and a steady stream of traffic. He pulled in some line, and the dragon rose a few feet—still not enough. His hands tingled with the effort of being patient; he wanted to reel in the line all at once and snatch the kite out of the sky. But if he didn't call the dragon back little by little, it might torpedo right into the traffic.

"Hiroshi!" Carlos's footsteps pounded up behind him. "Hey, cool kite."

"Thank you." Hiroshi kept his eyes trained on the dragon.

Carlos fell into step next to Hiroshi. "Ravi's bringing your grandfather over here." Hiroshi turned to see Ravi making his way down the path, guiding the wheelchair.

Bilal arrived next, out of breath "Is it gonna fall?"

Hiroshi reeled in a few more feet of line.

"Nah, it's going up—look at it!" Carlos pointed.

"Do you need help?" Bilal asked. "I've flown kites before, you know—me and my brother."

"Thanks." Hiroshi handed him the reel without taking his eyes off the kite. "Roll up the extra line. Don't let go."

Hiroshi took the line. Without the reel it was much easier to guide the kite now. The dragon drifted up and away from the traffic, but now Hiroshi had to coax it away from the grove of pine trees. If he could tempt the dragon into following a wide arc, he could bring it down without tangling the line in the trees. But the wind picked up, pushing the dragon closer and closer toward the pines.

Hiroshi hadn't realized Grandfather was there beside him until he heard his voice. "What do you think?"

Hiroshi glanced at Grandfather. "What do I think? I don't

know!" He couldn't keep the panic out of his words. "Help me get it down!"

"You know how to get it down, Hiroshi."

"No, I don't!" He offered the line to Grandfather, but Grandfather gently pushed Hiroshi's hands away.

"Look at the clouds. What do they tell you?"

As the kite drifted east, Hiroshi watched the clouds above it being carried west. "The wind changes direction higher up." Hiroshi allowed himself to hope.

"More line," he said, and Bilal unwound the reel. The kite climbed higher until it caught the westward wind. The dragon turned and chased after the clouds, leaving the trees behind.

"Well done, Hiroshi," Grandfather said.

"Man, that was awesome!" Carlos slapped Hiroshi on the back.

"Hey—look!" Bilal pointed. "It's going back out over the road."

Hiroshi spotted an open field on the other side of the street. "I can take it down over there, Grandfather. We need to cross the street."

"What now?" Ravi asked.

Hiroshi switched to English and pointed to the field. "I am going there. No trees."

"We'll help you." Carlos waved them toward the crosswalk.

Hiroshi nodded. "Ravi, can you—"

But Ravi was already gripping the handles of Grandfather's wheelchair. "I follow you." Ravi nodded.

Carlos crossed to the middle of the road and held up his hands. Cars from both directions came to a stop as Hiroshi stepped off the curb, eyes on the dragon. The kite flapped and dipped and followed Hiroshi across the street. Bilal trailed behind holding the reel, followed by Ravi and Grandfather.

When Hiroshi reached the curb, he stepped up and then pivoted, walking backward until he felt the pavement give way to spongy grass beneath his sneakers. As he pulled in the kite a few inches at a time, Bilal kept pace by winding up the extra line.

"Here it comes!" Carlos said.

"Where'd you get that kite?" Bilal asked.

"I made it." Hiroshi relaxed his shoulders—the dragon seemed to have given up the fight. "I made it, and my grandfather—he painted the dragon." The boys swung their heads in Grandfather's direction.

"Wow," Bilal said. "Cool."

Hiroshi lured the kite lower and lower until he could see the pout in the dragon's eyes. But before he could pluck it from the air, a river of wind swept the dragon to the left and spun it around. Disoriented, the dragon headed straight for the ground.

"It's going to crash!" Carlos yelled.

"I got it!" Ravi ran directly underneath the kite, holding his arms out.

"No, Ravi!" Hiroshi shouted. But he was too late.

Ravi lunged for the kite when it was just a few feet above the ground and grabbed one of the bamboo ribs. Ravi fell in an arc, his free arm waving in a circle. He landed with a thud, right on top of the dragon. They all heard the crunching and cracking of the bamboo ribs.

Hiroshi dropped his line and raced over.

Ravi rolled off the kite and stared at it like he wasn't sure how it got there. "I am so sorry."

Hiroshi ran his fingers over the kite, as if his light touch might hurt the dragon.

"Oh, man," Carlos said, shaking his head.

"It's not his fault, Hiroshi." Grandfather spoke softly, even though Hiroshi was the only one who understood his Japanese words. "He tried his best to save the kite."

"But now we can't fly it in the kite battle. And it's just a little over two weeks away."

"You can make a new kite, Hiroshi. You have time."

"Can you paint another dragon?"

"First build the kite, and then we'll worry about the design."

Bilal handed the reel to Hiroshi. "Man, sorry about your kite."

Hiroshi nodded, biting his lip. He took the kite from Ravi, who looked horrified. "Thank you for trying, Ravi."

Ravi shook his head. "I am sorry."

"It was not your fault."

Ravi shrugged, then opened his eyes wide. "I will help you make a new kite."

Hiroshi nodded. "Thank you."

But he didn't want Ravi's help. Grandfather was his only kite-making partner.

"It is time to go now, Hiroshi." Grandfather's eyelids were drooping, and Hiroshi realized he had to get him home. The boys said good-bye and headed back toward the park.

By the time they reached home, Grandfather had fallen asleep again. The dragon lay in his lap, defeated. Hiroshi knew it would never fly again.

Skye followed behind Hiroshi as he pushed Grandfather's wheel-chair through the crowd at the Cherry Blossom Festival. Grandfather pointed to something near the street vendors, and Hiroshi laughed. Even if she had been close enough to hear what they were saying and knew all the words they spoke, she probably wouldn't have understood. Their language wasn't just words; it was shared memories. Memories that she would never know. She heard her dad talking with Hiroshi's parents a few steps behind her—more memories of Japan.

Enough. Skye was tired of feeling left out. She tapped Hiroshi's shoulder. "Can I have a turn now?"

"Oh, I don't mind pushing." Hiroshi threw the words over his shoulder without even turning around. "I am not tired yet."

Skye slowed her step, then caught up with him again. "Really, I don't mind," she said through gritted teeth. She gripped one of the handles, leaving Hiroshi holding the other.

"Hey," Hiroshi said. "I've only been pushing for a little bit."

"A *little* bit?" She checked her watch. "You've had a turn for nineteen whole minutes!"

Grandfather glanced back and looked surprised to see them

176

side by side. "I'm glad you decided to work together." He smiled and turned back around.

Skye and Hiroshi narrowed their eyes at each other.

"You'll need that kind of cooperation on the day of the kite battle," Grandfather said.

Skye and Hiroshi pushed the chair in silence through the grilled smell of *yakitori,* the sound of Japanese spoken by strangers, and women wrapped in flowered silk kimonos. Skye could be enjoying all of this if it weren't for Hiroshi the Wheelchair Hog.

Finally Grandfather broke the silence. "Hiroshi could use an extra set of hands if the new kite is to be ready in time."

Skye saw Hiroshi stiffen. "I bet my dad would help," Skye said. "I can ask him."

Grandfather glanced back at her and smiled. "I was thinking of you, Sorano-chan."

"Me? But I've never built a kite before. My dad would be much better at it."

There was no way she was going to be Hiroshi's kite-building assistant. She didn't even know if she'd survive being his kite-battle assistant. He'd probably boss her around, tell her where to go, when to roll up the line, when to let it out. And then if they didn't win, he'd blame her. But she could never tell Grandfather that.

"Everyone must begin somewhere, Sorano-chan." Grandfather turned and looked at Hiroshi. "You can build the kite, of course, but it would be good for Sorano to watch. One day she will be a great help to you." When Hiroshi nodded, Grandfather smiled and faced front again.

Hiroshi stepped back, leaving the handle free for Skye. She

took both handles and kept walking. Good. It was her turn, anyway. She knew Hiroshi must be mad at her—again. But it wasn't her fault that Grandfather wanted to include her. Later she'd tell Hiroshi that he could build his own stupid kite. And she'd be his assistant in the kite battle, but only because she'd promised Grandfather. Then she'd leave Hiroshi alone, like he wanted.

Skye shook her head. She wasn't about to let Hiroshi ruin this day. "Grandfather?" she said. "Can you tell another story about Grandmother?"

He turned and smiled. "I would be honored. Why don't we pull over and you can take a rest?"

Skye spotted a bench up ahead. "How about there?"

"That would be perfect," Grandfather said.

Hiroshi went to tell his parents they were stopping, then came jogging over. He pointed at a drink stand across the street. "They're going to get extra water, so we can wait here." Skye's mom waved from the stand and Skye waved back.

"Well, then," Grandfather said. "For today's story, I've chosen one that even Hiroshi has not heard. But the time has come to share it." Skye settled on the bench as far from Hiroshi as possible, with Grandfather facing them both.

"When I was a young boy growing up in my village," he began, "I spent all my free time with a kite string in my hand. The wind was my teacher, and I paid attention to its lessons. It taught me to be both a better kite maker and *rokkaku* flier.

"One girl from the village named Mariko saw me making a kite one day and asked if I would teach her how to make one. I agreed, and she proved to be a quick study. She was precise and patient in her work, essential qualities for a kite maker. Before long, I could not tell the difference between her kites and my own.

"She might have felt pride in her new skill, but she was restless. She wanted me to teach her how to fly the kites. Not just for play, mind you. She wanted to become a kite fighter.

"At first I laughed: why would she want to learn a boy's game? But she didn't smile. Instead she asked, 'What brings more pleasure—kite fighting or learning the proper way to pour tea?'

"That settled that. The next day we went up on the hill for her first flying lesson. Before we launched the kite, I spoke many words about wind direction, speed, and the will of a kite. After a few minutes of this, she said, 'Enough. I want to fly.'

"And fly she did. She was a natural. There were some things I found difficult to explain, such as how to launch when the wind is just so or how to pull the kite out of a wind stall. I just did what felt right. As it turned out I did not need to explain these things to her. She felt it, too, and the wind became her friend.

"Once she could launch the kite on her own, I showed her every one of my *rokkaku* tricks. After a year or so, I knew she could beat most of the other kite fighters in our village. When the date for the annual *rokkaku* battle was announced, she wanted to enter. We both knew she couldn't—girls were not allowed to enter kite battles in those days. But she was determined. She decided to dress as a boy and enter anyway. I lent her some of my younger brother's clothes, complete with a hat that shaded her eyes from the sun, and hid her long braid from the judges.

"This was my second battle, and everyone expected me to win again. But this time some older boys from a nearby village had entered, and I was nervous. I had never faced them in competition

179

before, but I knew of their reputations. They usually entered the bigger battles, on the main island, and brought back trophies.

"Looking back I remember the kites more than their fliers. Some kites had special words painted on them for luck. A few had complicated designs—a carp, or the face of a folktale warrior. Other kites had only one color, like Mariko's—hers was a pale yellow, the color of courage.

"My kite was simple. After so many hours giving flying lessons that year, I did not have time to paint anything elaborate. My kite was white, with a large red circle painted off-center—the symbol of a winking dragon.

"During the battle, I had some near misses; my kite almost went down several times. In the end, the kites of those who could read the wind were spared. When four kites remained I saw that Mariko's kite was one of them. I was pleased she was doing so well, especially in her first battle. In no time two other kites had fallen from the sky, leaving only my kite and Mariko's kite hanging on the wind.

"My happiness for her ended in the pit of my stomach. I had known she would do well but never guessed she would have come this far. I had avoided her kite earlier, as I did not want to be the one to eliminate her from the competition. But now I had no choice. I only hoped she would not be too angry with me.

"To keep her honor, I decided not to knock her kite out of the sky right away. By this time the crowd was yelling my name, clapping and cheering. No one yelled Mariko's name, as no one recognized her. The crowd's good wishes rushed in through my ears and went straight to my head. I began to show off, performing tricks with my kite, which brought even more shouts and applause.

180

"And then it happened. Mariko's kite came in fast—too fast for me to react. Her kite tipped mine in one fluid movement and sent it straight into the ground.

"Mariko had won, and I had lost.

"The crowd stood silent at first. Then they all politely clapped for the winner. Mariko turned to me and bowed, as was the tradition. I returned the bow, if only to hide my red face. I had never felt so ashamed. Mariko walked over to the judges' stand to accept her prize. She bowed to each judge, and the medallion was placed around her neck. She then headed toward home, away from the crowd, before anyone could recognize her. My competitors' glee was apparent on their faces, as was the disappointment of neighbors who had boasted that I would win. I felt that I had shamed my village.

"As I walked toward the judges' stand, I was trying not to think; I did not want my heart to talk me out of what I had decided to do. When I approached the judges and bowed, I almost turned and walked away. But anger and humiliation were stronger than friendship that day, and the words rushed out—almost on their own: 'The winner is a girl.'

"I am not proud of what I did in that moment. And things only became worse once those words had escaped my mouth. The head judge rose and followed Mariko home. When he discovered where she lived, he knocked on the door and explained the situation to her parents. She had to give up the medallion. Her parents said she had dishonored their family by lying and entering a contest meant for boys.

"A few days later the head judge came to my home and presented the medallion to me. By then I did not want it, but I accepted the medallion so I could return it to Mariko. But she did not want it back. I was crushed.

"That was the year after the war ended, and times were hard in our village. Her family went to live with relatives north in Hokkaido, and I feared I would never see her again. But seven years later her family returned. When I heard the news, I went to her door and asked her father's permission to take her for a walk. Our parents had been friends, so her father agreed. But he always followed fifteen paces behind us.

"When I offered my apologies again to her, she accepted with words but not with her heart. I came every day to ask her father if I might take her for a walk, and each day he accepted. I wanted her forgiveness, but I could not say too much for fear that her father would overhear. So I made her a miniature kite, the size of her palm. On the kite I had painted the *kanji* for *apology*. She took it and tucked it into the sleeve of her kimono but said nothing.

"The next day I went to her house, but her father said that she was not feeling well. I came back the next day and the next. Finally, after seven days, she appeared. She said nothing as we began our walk, but when we heard her father behind us pause to talk to a neighbor, she slipped a miniature kite into my hand, quick as a dragonfly. I was devastated, thinking she had returned my kite and my apology.

"After a few minutes had passed, she said, 'Perhaps you might look at what is written.' When I opened my hand, I saw that the kite was not mine. It was a new kite, the craftsmanship far superior to my own. I turned it over, and saw the *kanji* for *new beginnings*.

"There have been few times in my life when my heart has soared as high.

"The next year we were married. I had no money to buy a proper wedding gift. So on our wedding day, I offered her the medallion that should have been hers all those years ago. I told her that it was not a true gift, since it had never belonged to me. But she cried and laughed and wore it around her neck for the rest of her days.

Skye sat still, not wanting to break the spell.

"Why have you never told me that story, Grandfather?" Hiroshi asked.

Grandfather sighed. "I suppose it is because I am not proud of the way I acted. Your grandmother was a gift, a gift that I almost missed." Grandfather grew quiet, and Skye knew he was missing Grandmother. She wished she'd known Grandmother so she could miss her, too.

寛 ○

After Grandfather's story they all headed toward the cherry trees that surrounded the Tidal Basin. Hiroshi would not have minded if Skye accidentally fell into the basin. Or maybe he could tie her to a kite, launch her into the air, and cut the string, letting the wind carry her somewhere—anywhere—far away. He'd heard about people hundreds of years ago attaching themselves to kites; maybe there was a way to convince Skye to try it.

Why hadn't Grandfather ever told him that story about Grandmother? He'd said it was because he was ashamed of how he had acted all those years ago. But Hiroshi would have forgiven Grandfather for anything.

Hiroshi heard Skye answer a soccer question for Grandfather, who looked fascinated by her every word. Better to catch up with Father and First Uncle, who were walking ahead. As Hiroshi passed Skye, he heard Grandfather say, "The wind looks good today."

Grandfather looked straight at Hiroshi and then winked. When Hiroshi didn't answer, Grandfather continued. "Today would be a perfect day for the battle." Without looking at Skye, Hiroshi slowed his pace to match Grandfather's chair.

"Two weeks to go," Hiroshi said. "We'll just have to be patient."

184

Grandfather tapped his fingers in time to the music of the bands parading down Constitution Avenue. The marching tubas and trumpets taunted Hiroshi with their American music, reminding him how far from home he was.

As they waited to cross the street, Hiroshi noticed the fragile pink cherry blossom trees reflected in the water of the Tidal Basin. There must be hundreds of trees—maybe more than a thousand.

"*Sakura*," Skye said. "They're beautiful."

"They're also useful," Hiroshi was surprised that his voice came out wistful instead of angry. It was like he'd forgotten that he was talking to Skye.

"Useful?" Skye looked curious. "Do they make things from the petals?"

Grandfather chuckled. "Perhaps some do. But kite fighters have a unique appreciation for the blossoms."

"Look at them now," Hiroshi said, pointing to a handful of falling blossoms fluttering away in the breeze. "You can tell which direction the wind is blowing over there." Hiroshi watched the wind lift the blossoms eastward. It seemed like the rising sun was calling them home, back to Japan.

Grandfather's voice was soft. "If the dragon were flying today, the blossoms' path would give us clues to the fickle wind's plans." He turned to Hiroshi. "Why don't we visit the trees up close?"

First Uncle frowned. "There are a lot of people at the Tidal Basin, Father. I'm not sure your chair will get through."

Grandfather smiled. "Hiroshi and Sorano will have no problem, I am sure. The *sakura* are best viewed from up close."

"Here," Skye said, stepping back. "You can have a turn, if you want." That was all the permission Hiroshi needed, and he guided

Grandfather's chair across the street and onto the crowded path that ringed the Tidal Basin.

For once Skye didn't bug him about pushing the wheelchair again; she seemed mesmerized by the pink cherry trees. "I've never seen them up close before," she said, her voice almost a whisper.

"Never?" Grandfather looked at First Uncle like he couldn't believe it.

First Uncle looked sheepish. "We, ah, used to come when Skye—Sorano—was little. Then I guess soccer games sort of took over our weekends."

Sakura were everywhere in Japan; how strange that Skye had never seen one of these trees up close. Hiroshi had thought Skye didn't care about Japanese things. But one glance at First Uncle's red face told Hiroshi that maybe it wasn't all Skye's fault.

People made way for the wheelchair, and Hiroshi kept going until Grandfather held up his hand to stop. "That one is a beauty." Grandfather pointed to a giant cherry tree, boughs heavy with delicate blossoms. It canopied over the sidewalk and the strolling crowd, brushing the water with the tips of its branches.

Mother smiled and put her hand on Hiroshi's shoulder. "It is lovely, isn't it?"

"*Hanami* is different here," Hiroshi said.

"*Hanami*—that's when people go to look at the cherry blossoms, right?" Skye asked. Hiroshi nodded. "How is it different?"

Hiroshi shrugged. "People here are walking by, but not many stop to sit beneath the trees."

Skye frowned. "Maybe Americans don't know that's what they're supposed to do."

Grandfather smiled. "We know what to do, don't we?" He

186

winked at his sons, and they pulled out a blanket from First Uncle's backpack. Father and First Uncle spread the blanket on the ground, opened their arms, and grinned. "Now for the food."

Mother and Aunt Cathy opened another pack and pulled out cups and containers with dumplings. They set everything up in the center of the blanket.

"Father, would you like to sit on the blanket?" Hiroshi's father asked.

"I can help you, if you'd like," Hiroshi offered.

"Me, too," Skye chimed in.

"Thank you all for your offer, but I am comfortable right here." Grandfather smiled. "But the rest of you should sit." He turned to Hiroshi and Skye. "You must be tired from all that walking and chair pushing."

"Oh, we're not tired." Hiroshi realized he'd answered for Skye, too, but she nodded along with him.

"We'll keep you company," Skye said, leaning against the great gnarled trunk.

"Sure we will," Hiroshi added. While Mother and Father talked with Skye's parents on the blanket, Hiroshi brought some dumplings to Grandfather.

"Thank you, Hiroshi. They look delicious." But by the time Hiroshi was on his second dumpling, Grandfather hadn't even touched his.

"Heads up!" a voice called out. Hiroshi ducked just in time as a Frisbee sliced through the air over his head. It met the cherry tree with a rustle and a crack, then fell at Hiroshi's feet.

"Sorry about that." A teenage boy jogged up to him. "You okay?"

Hiroshi picked up the Frisbee and handed it to the boy. "I'm fine. No problem."

"Thanks, man." The boy jogged away with the Frisbee in hand.

"Oh, no!"

Hiroshi turned to see Skye pointing to a twig of blossoms that had fallen onto Grandfather's knee.

"Look what they did with their Frisbee!" She looked as if she were about to cry.

Hiroshi didn't know why she was so upset. This tree must have thousands of blossoms, and there must be a thousand trees around the Tidal Basin. What difference did three small blossoms make?

Grandfather picked up the sprig. "As beautiful as the blossoms are, they are also very fragile. In two weeks' time these flowers will all be gone." Grandfather smiled. "We should not mourn their departure, Sorano-chan. The blossoms are a sign of spring, a promise of beauty yet to come."

He handed the blossoms to Skye. "They return each year, like clockwork. You can depend on that." Skye nodded and tucked them carefully into her jacket's wide front pocket.

The breeze moved through the branches above, and more blossoms fell around them before the wind snatched them away. The wind had always been Hiroshi's friend, something he depended on to lift his kite and keep it floating on the air. But now he wished the wind would leave the trees alone. It was true that the blossoms could last as long as two weeks, but Hiroshi had seen high winds and rain rip them from their branches in only a few days.

It had never mattered to Hiroshi how long the blossoms stayed. But now he didn't want them to blow away. He wanted them to stay forever.

188

Skye was thrilled when Grandfather finally insisted she help with the new kite. This was her chance to make up for almost ruining the dragon kite. Every day she'd race to Hiroshi's house from soccer practice. They'd been following the same routine faithfully for the past week: grab a quick snack from Aunt Naoko, then head to the basement workshop with their backpacks. They were supposed to be doing homework, but the new kite needed to be made. It needed to be perfect, and it needed to be finished in time.

In time for the kite battle. In time for Grandfather to see it fly.

Skye and Hiroshi always spoke in Japanese whenever they were in the workshop. When Hiroshi taught her the kite-making rules, she liked to imagine the same words coming from Grandfather in his faraway workshop in Japan:

> *Your measurements must be exact.*
> *Poor planning makes for sloppy flying.*
> *A good frame should be perfectly symmetrical.*
> *Attach the strings of the bridle with care, and you will*
> *be repaid with a kite that flies on its own.*

They reported their progress to Grandfather each evening

189

before Skye went home for dinner. They told him what stage the kite was in and what the plan was for the next day. Sometimes Grandfather was awake for their daily report, and some days he wasn't.

On Friday evening they were almost ready.

"It'll be ready to paint tomorrow." Hiroshi tapped the *washi* paper near the bamboo frame. "It feels solid."

"I can't believe we actually made a kite." Well, Hiroshi had done most of the making, but Skye was proud that she'd been able to help. "I'll come over tomorrow right after my exams, and we can paint it."

"And then we'll show it to Grandfather."

Skye couldn't wait to make him proud.

When Skye woke the next day, her first thought was the kite. Her next thought was the exams. She threw off her covers and saw her Japanese grammar book lying on her bedside table. Next to the book was a good-luck card from Amber. She felt a pang of guilt when she realized she hadn't thought about soccer in over a week. But she'd have more time for soccer once she passed her exams. If she passed her exams.

She knew Grandfather was proud of Hiroshi—after all, he was a kite maker and flier just like Grandfather. But was Grandfather proud of Skye? He had never seen her play soccer. He had been patient with her less-than-perfect Japanese. The exams were her chance to make him proud of her, too.

Skye got out of bed. She would pass these exams.

On her way downstairs with the grammar book tucked under

her arm, Skye mentally recited verb conjugations. Every few steps she peeked in her book to check if she'd gotten them right. She had.

"Mom?"

"I'm in the kitchen, honey."

Skye didn't know if she could stomach anything for breakfast. Maybe she would just grab something after she got dressed and eat in the car. She came around the corner into the kitchen and stopped short at the sight of her parents. They were sitting at the table with cups of coffee and looked as if they hadn't slept all night. Her mom's eyes were rimmed in red.

She wanted to ask, but before she could open her mouth, she knew.

"Skye," her dad began. And then the air seemed to drain right out of him. Her mom put her arm around him and pulled him close, then held out a hand to Skye.

But Skye was frozen. "It's Grandfather, isn't it?"

Her mom nodded, fresh tears spilling down her cheeks. "Yes, honey. He died during the night."

Skye's heart pounded in her ears. "But . . . we haven't finished the kite. He hasn't seen it yet." She wondered if she had spoken aloud or if the words were trapped in her head.

Her dad went to put his arm around her, then led her to a chair. He took her Japanese book and laid it on the table. Skye stared at the picture of the Japanese cartoon children smiling on the cover of her textbook. Why were they smiling?

Her dad picked up the phone. "I'll call your Japanese teacher and postpone your exams."

"No." The word flew from Skye's mouth before she'd had a chance to think. She hadn't made Grandfather proud. But she would.

"I'm taking the exams."

Hiroshi didn't know what had woken him with a start so early in the morning. He sat up in bed, wide awake, and looked around his room. The morning light had already begun to play at the edges of his window shade. Pushing aside his covers, he got up and walked over to the window. When he tugged at the shade, it rolled up with a snap.

Something didn't feel right. Not a single leaf swayed on the branches of the tree outside his window. Nothing stirred in the early sunlight. The wind had ceased.

He heard the low sound of Father's voice. Opening his door a crack, he heard Mother's voice, but he still couldn't make out any words. Something about their hushed tones kept his feet from making a sound on the stairs. They probably didn't want to wake Grandfather.

"Yes, yes, I called the rest of the family. They can be here in two days." Father sounded tired. "No, he's still asleep. And Sorano?"

Hiroshi crept closer to the bottom of the stairs. Father said good-bye to the person on the other end of the line, then hung up. Hiroshi stood there, ready to walk into the kitchen.

Mother's soft crying stopped him mid-step. Father murmured

something to Mother, then, "Let's go onto the deck so we don't wake Hiroshi."

Hiroshi heard the back door open, then Mother's words: "I cannot believe he is gone." And then the door shut behind them.

Hiroshi froze. He raced back up the stairs to Grandfather's room and flung the door open. Grandfather's futon was empty.

It couldn't be true—Hiroshi wasn't ready yet. He and Skye hadn't finished the kite, and they hadn't tested it and hadn't painted it, and the kite battle—

Hiroshi flew out of Grandfather's room and down the basement steps into Grandfather's workshop. Without turning on the light, he stood in the middle of the room. Grandfather's workshop was lit only by the sun filtering in through the high, small windows. He took a deep, quivery breath and closed his eyes.

The smell of bamboo still hung in the air. He pretended he was standing in Grandfather's workshop in Japan. Grandfather would come in any minute now, eager to get started on the next kite.

He opened his eyes. Everything was in its place; the paints on the shelves, the brushes, the stacks of *washi* paper, and the kite that he and Skye had been working on all week. And there was the magnificent dragon kite. He removed it from its place on the wall. Hiroshi didn't care about the broken bamboo and the rip that Ravi had made—it was still Grandfather's masterpiece.

But wait—Hiroshi peered at the kite, then turned it over and inspected the underside. The bamboo pole had been replaced with a new one, and the dragon had been repainted. Grandfather must have done all this while Hiroshi had been at school. But how could he have fixed it when he'd always been so tired?

The silence was broken by the tapping of a rosebush branch against one of the high windows. Hiroshi went and stood below the windows, looking at the sky—a bright blue interrupted only by a few puffs of billowy clouds gliding by.

The wind had arrived.

It was a perfect day for flying kites.

Skye's pencil hadn't stopped moving for a full three hours. Her hand was starting to cramp, and she ached to stretch her fingers. But she couldn't stop. She couldn't stop, because the more she wrote, the more Japanese words—verbs, nouns, rules, adjectives, more rules—swirled inside her head. History, reading, calligraphy. More words meant fewer thoughts that could creep from her heart into her head.

"Time."

Kumamoto Sensei's voice echoed over everyone's heads. The sound of pencils hitting desks sounded like firecrackers, and Skye jumped, pencil still in hand. Kumamoto Sensei's glare forced Skye's pencil to her desk. Skye had insisted that her dad drop her off at school without talking to Kumamoto Sensei. Skye could only hold herself together if no one knew, if everything was business as usual.

"Boys and girls, the written exam is now complete." Kumamoto Sensei nodded toward another Japanese teacher who was collecting the exams from students' desks. "As you know, Takahashi Sensei is the instructor for the advanced class. If you pass, you will have the honor of becoming one of his pupils for the afternoon summer session."

Skye didn't look at Takahashi Sensei as he collected her paper.

195

She had seen his gentle face before, and today she didn't want to see any kindness. She even avoided Maya's looks from across the room.

"Takahashi Sensei will be joining us in the exam room to evaluate the written portions of your exam while I administer your oral exam. You will be given your exam results immediately." Kumamoto Sensei picked up a clipboard and pen from her desk. "Now, who would like to go first?"

No one moved. Then Skye rose and stood beside her desk. "I would like to go first, Sensei."

The other kids turned to look at her as if she were crazy. Surprise flickered across Kumamoto Sensei's face for a moment, then her stern mask snapped back in place.

"Very well, Tsuki-san. You may come with me." Skye gathered her things and followed her teacher into the hall. She knew this would be a good time to run over the list of verbs in her head, but she suddenly felt tired. She put one foot in front of the other until they reached an office.

"*Dozo.*" Kumamoto Sensei gestured toward a chair, and Skye sat, placing her jacket on the empty chair next to her. Her teacher moved a few papers from a desk to a side table and sat in the chair opposite Skye. "Shall we begin?"

What am I doing? Skye thought. *Why did I volunteer to go first?* Her breath quickened, but she couldn't do anything to slow it down.

"Would you like a drink of water before we begin?"

Skye nodded. "*Hai. Arigato gozaimasu.*"

Takahashi Sensei appeared at her side with a paper cup of water. "Relax, Tsuki-san. It is only a test." Skye looked up at him.

His kind face reminded her of another such face. She braced herself for the tears, but they didn't come. Instead, calm washed over her. She could do this.

She took a sip of water, thanked the teacher again, and set the cup on the desk. "I am ready."

"*Hai,* Tsuki-san. Let us begin."

For the next twenty minutes, Skye was asked about her favorite foods, school activities, and the ins and outs of the Japanese tea ceremony. Skye spoke without remembering what she said, all the while wrapped in her blanket of calm. She saw Kumamoto Sensei make notes in her book, but Skye didn't care.

Finally Kumamoto Sensei announced, "For the last question tell me about a favorite hobby. Please describe the last time you participated in this activity so that you may utilize the past tense." Last week, Skye had planned to talk about soccer. But now she spoke of kites and bamboo and wind and string. The hill in the park. How to make a fighting kite.

When she finished, Kumamoto Sensei blinked, then rose to join Takahashi Sensei. The teachers leaned over Skye's written exams, and she waited. Her blanket of calm slipped away, and Skye wrapped her arms around herself to keep from shaking. When the teachers came back, Takahashi Sensei glanced sideways at Kumamoto Sensei.

Skye wanted them to tell her that she had passed. She didn't know how she'd gotten through the exams; she barely remembered her answers. But she wanted to pass. Not just for the All-Star team. She wanted her grade to show that she was worthy of being Japanese. Worthy of being the granddaughter of Shou Tsuki, respected kite maker, renowned kite fighter, beloved Grandfather.

"Tsuki-san," Kumamoto Sensei began. "Never in my twenty-five years of teaching have I seen results like these."

Skye looked at her knees. She had failed. Failed herself—her Japanese self. Failed Grandfather. She didn't want to hear anymore, so she stood to go. But when she looked up at Kumamoto Sensei, her teacher was smiling. At her. Skye sat back down.

"You passed, Tsuki-san."

Skye stared at her teacher. The smile was still there.

"Tsuki-san, I had never heard you speak Japanese without being afraid. Until now. Today you had no fear. For your oral exam, I give you a perfect score."

Skye blinked. *A perfect score?*

Takahashi Sensei laughed. "I am surprised I was able to concentrate on grading your written exams. I assure you it was difficult once you began talking about *rokkaku*—kite fighting brings back fond childhood memories." He folded Skye's stapled exams and handed the packet to her like it was a secret document. "Of course there were a few grammatical errors."

Skye stared at the folded papers. She didn't have perfect scores. And Kumamoto Sensei had said she'd need an almost perfect final score to pass into Takahashi Sensei's advanced class next semester. *Was it close enough?*

He nodded. "You did have some minor errors in each subject, but they did not detract from your overall grade—it is nothing we cannot fix in my class next semester." He smiled. Skye opened her exams to see her final score on the cover page. At the top was a red three, the highest score possible. She bowed deeply and thanked her teachers—present and future—then turned to go.

"Tsuki-san," Kumamoto Sensei called out, "your jacket." She pointed to the chair.

Skye took her jacket, bowed again and left the quiet room. She walked out the double doors and sat on the bench in front of the flagpoles to wait for her dad. Usually she called him right after class to say she was ready. He'd be sitting in the coffee shop down the road now reading the newspaper, like he always did while waiting for her call.

Skye unzipped her front jacket pocket, reached in, and pulled out her cell phone. But something else brushed her fingers—silk and wood. Reaching in with her other hand, she pulled out a twig with three perfect cherry blossoms. Not taking her eyes off of the sprig, she set the phone on the bench beside her. These must have been the blossoms that Grandfather had given her a week ago. But that was impossible—the fragile flowers should have withered and died after a week in her jacket pocket.

But there they were, as fresh and delicate and pink as if they had just been picked. Skye twirled the twig in her fingers, and her eyes filled with tears until all she could see was a blurred cloud of pink against dark cherry wood.

Over the next few days, Hiroshi felt as if he were moving under-water. Relatives traveled from Japan, some of whom he'd never met before. They all spoke in low voices, bowing deeply to Father. Aunt Cathy had invited Hiroshi to join her and Skye on a walk, but he told her he had to help Mother. That wasn't really true, but he wanted to be alone—not easy when he was constantly surrounded by people.

"Why don't you go ride your bike, Hiroshi?" Mother had said when she found him sitting on the stairs. "It's a beautiful day out-side. Go get some fresh air."

Hiroshi didn't feel like riding his bike. Or going outside. Or staying inside. He walked past Father and heard him talking with Third Uncle in the hallway about the white kimono.

Hiroshi wandered outside and sank onto the front step. The white kimono. This would be the one they placed in the casket along with sandals, leggings, and a headband with a triangle in the center. Paper money would also be laid in the casket—Grandfather might need the money to get to the next world. His favorite things from this life could also be added to the casket for his next life. Everything would be cremated together before Grandfather began his journey.

Favorite things.

Hiroshi stood up. He knew what he had to do. There wasn't much time, with the wake scheduled for tomorrow.

Hiroshi hurried back inside the house and weaved his way through the crowd of relatives and down the basement steps. Overhead, muffled voices mingled with creaking floorboards as people padded from room to room in their slippers. Hiroshi breathed in the peace of Grandfather's workshop.

He walked straight over to the box of bamboo and chose a few of the smallest pieces from the stack. Still too big. One by one, he trimmed them down to size; some the length of his hand, others no longer than his little finger. With a thick-bladed knife, he sliced the bamboo along its grain until each piece was thin enough. The light outside began to fade, but he kept working.

He didn't hear Mother come down the stairs, and jumped when she set a plate of rice cakes on the worktable beside him. "You must be hungry, Hiroshi. You've been down here for almost two hours. Are you all right?"

"*Hai*. I'm just making something for Grandfather. You know, for the wake tomorrow."

"Don't stay up too late. Tomorrow will be a long day for all of us."

Hiroshi listened to her footsteps as she climbed back up the stairs. Rubbing his stiff neck, he stood to stretch. The creaking floorboards and low voices had faded. He popped a rice cake into his mouth and sat back down to work. He measured and cut the *washi* paper to fit the dimensions of the bamboo sticks, then opened the bottle of glue.

An hour later Father came downstairs. "Son, it's time for bed."

201

"Look, Father. I think it's finally finished." Hiroshi held a miniature, six-sided *rokkaku* kite, complete with string.

"Hiro-chan, did you make that yourself?"

"The glue still has to dry, but it'll be ready by tomorrow."

Father leaned in to inspect the kite. "It's exquisite, Son."

"I didn't have time to paint it, but the kimono and other things will be white, so I thought this could be white, too."

"He would be so proud of you." Father sat on the stool next to Hiroshi. "He was already so proud of you."

"Do you ever wish you had become a kite maker, like Grand-father?"

Father smiled a faraway smile. "When I was a boy, I used to think I would. I loved flying kites just as much as you do. But I was nowhere near as good as you are. Grandfather knew it, too, although he was always patient with me. My younger brother was even worse than I was, if you can believe that. First Uncle had Grandfather's talent, but once he fell in love with Aunt Cathy, he left kites and Japan behind him."

"Was Grandfather sad that no one wanted to help him in his workshop?"

"He may have been, but he never showed it. When I finally admitted to him that I had no future in kites, he reminded me that one does not need to be a champion to fly a kite for pleasure. He encouraged us to become whatever we wanted but to always leave room for fun."

Hiroshi held the tiny kite up to the light. "He's got to have a kite in his next life, you know. And maybe this will help him to remember me." He gently set the kite on the table.

Father rested his hand on Hiroshi's shoulder. "Hiro-chan, Grandfather won't need a kite to remember you."

Hiroshi hoped Father was right. When they got to the top of the stairs, Hiroshi took one more look at the tiny kite alone on the worktable. "You can go ahead, Father. I'll be right there."

Hiroshi went back down the steps, picked up the cloud white kite and carried it back upstairs. When he got to his room, he set it next to the photo of himself with Grandfather. When Hiroshi finally fell asleep, the white kite drifted in and out of his dreams.

If Skye had to smile and bow at another relative she didn't know, she decided she would bow herself right out the door and walk home. Everyone had gathered at Hiroshi's house for the wake, but all they did was pay attention to her. What was her favorite subject in school? How did she like living in America? Had she been play-ing soccer long?

Skye had her own question: Why couldn't everyone just leave her alone? Whenever she overheard snippets of stories about Grandfather, she'd edge closer, hoping for a Grandfather story that she could tuck into her heart. But as soon as they saw her, they'd smile and she'd bow and they'd ask her another school question.

Skye needed some air. But when she opened the door, she found a man no taller than she was standing on the front step in a dark grey robe, his hand poised to knock.

Aunt Naoko rushed past her. "*Dozo.*"

Skye opened the door wider, and Aunt Naoko invited the man in, announcing that the priest had arrived. He stepped into the foyer, setting off a flurry of bowing from the others. Skye sighed and closed the door, wishing she were standing on the other side of it.

The doorbell rang again, and this time Skye's dad answered it. The guest offered him a white envelope wrapped with thin black and white ribbons. Skye wondered what was in the envelopes, but she couldn't ask her dad in front of the guest. When she saw Hiroshi come in from outside, she went over to ask him.

"It's *koden,* condolence money for the family," Hiroshi explained. "You don't have this tradition?"

Skye shook her head. "Is it supposed to make us feel any better? Because if it is, it's not working."

"I know." Hiroshi looked as miserable as Skye felt.

Her dad waved them over as the guests filed into the living room. Skye spotted the tablet on the altar and nudged Hiroshi. "I know my Japanese isn't perfect, but that's not Grandfather's name."

Hiroshi whispered back, "It's the *kaimyo*—the name the priest inscribed on the tablet. Another tradition."

"So it's the priest's name?"

"No, it's Grandfather's new name."

Skye frowned. "Why does he need a new name?"

"It's for his next life. He's supposed to follow a path leading across the Sanzu River. Now that he has a new name, his spirit won't come back whenever we use his old name; he'll keep following the path."

Skye shook her head. "But I don't want his spirit to go away. I want him to stay."

"Me, too." Hiroshi sighed. "Father says we're supposed to come home from the funeral parlor using a different route from the one we use to get there. So Grandfather's spirit won't get confused and follow us home."

Who cares about tradition? Skye thought. She had an idea. "So what if we don't?" She raised an eyebrow.

"Don't what?"

"Take a different path?"

A slow grin spread across Hiroshi's face. "We can ride our bikes back home."

Skye nodded. "The funeral parlor isn't far from the park, and we ride our bikes there all the time."

"Skye, Hiroshi—" Her mom put her hands on their shoulders. "We're about to begin."

Everyone was kneeling on cushions in front of the altar, which was piled with fruit and flowers. Skye knelt between her parents. Chin down, she snuck a peek at the open casket. She couldn't see inside from where she was kneeling, which was good; she wasn't sure if she wanted to see Grandfather this way.

The priest came into the room, and everyone stopped whispering. Facing the altar, the priest bowed, lit some incense, and began the reading. One by one, family members approached the casket. As Grandfather's eldest sons, Skye's dad and Hiroshi's father went first. They bowed before adding incense to an urn, then bowed again before returning to their places. Their younger brothers rose and approached the casket.

Skye's mom squeezed her hand. "You don't have to go up if you don't want to," she whispered. Skye wasn't sure. Maybe it was better to remember Grandfather as he used to be, smiling and gentle.

"If I go, how do I know when it's my turn?"

Her mom whispered back, "The sons go first, then the wives, then the children."

Skye's uncles returned to their cushions, and their wives and Hiroshi's mother stood. Skye's mom stayed on her cushion.

"Mom, aren't you going?"

She nodded. "I think I'm supposed to follow the others, since

I've only known—knew—him a short while." Her eyes filled with tears. "I wish I could have had more time with him."

Skye squeezed her mom's hand. Three pairs of women's slippers stopped in front of her mom's knees. When Skye looked up, her aunts smiled, inviting her mom to come with them.

"Oh." Her mom looked flustered, but then she nodded and smiled and got up to join them.

Skye watched carefully so she would know what to do if she decided to go. Hiroshi would go next, so she had time to decide. But once her mom returned with the aunts, Hiroshi came over and stood next to Skye. She looked up, and he nodded toward the casket. "We're next," he whispered.

He was waiting for her. She couldn't not go. So she stood on shaky legs and followed Hiroshi's lead as he bowed, offered incense, and then walked up to the casket. When she finally saw Grandfather, Skye almost smiled in relief. He looked like he always did, except his eyes were closed and he wore a cloud-white kimono.

"Look for us later on our bikes, Grandfather," she whispered.

Hiroshi nodded. "We'll show you the way back home."

A flash of white in Hiroshi's hand caught Skye's eye. He laid a tiny kite on the white kimono that was folded next to Grandfather. Then she remembered and slipped her hand into her pocket. She fingered the soft petals of the cherry blossoms as she pulled them out of her pocket, then laid the sprig next to Hiroshi's kite. "*Arigato gozaimasu*, Grandfather. Thank you." She released the cherry blossom stem and took a small step back next to Hiroshi, who smiled at her.

"Now we're supposed to bow," he whispered.

She smiled back through tears, then bowed her deepest bow.

宽 ◯

A few hours later Hiroshi and Skye rode their bikes back from the funeral parlor. They didn't speak the whole way home, but the silence between them wasn't angry, for once. The wind was gentle, and Hiroshi pedaled slowly, careful to retrace the same path the family had taken earlier.

When they arrived at his house, Hiroshi and Skye headed straight for the basement workshop. They still had to paint the kite and then test it.

Skye picked up the plain white kite. "What if it doesn't fly?"

"It will fly." Hiroshi's voice sounded more confident than he felt. The kite had to fly. There wasn't time to make a new one before the competition. Hiroshi had promised Grandfather that he and Skye would enter the contest; he would keep that promise.

Skye set the kite down and walked over to the shelves of paint. "What kind of design do you want to paint?"

Hiroshi looked at the dragon kite hanging on the wall. Its eyes didn't look fierce anymore—just empty. *I'm sorry you can't fly in the competition*, Hiroshi thought. *We'd win for sure with you at the end of our string.* But he couldn't risk losing the dragon if it crashed in the battle. He went to the new kite and inspected it. The glue had dried, the bamboo ribs looked straight, and the *washi* paper fit the frame precisely. It looked good. The line was tied on tight, and the wooden dragon reel was ready. But would the kite fly?

Skye set a jar of brushes on the table next to the kite. "Can you paint another dragon?"

Hiroshi sighed. "I'd like to, but it would never look like Grandfather's."

Skye nodded. "I know what you mean."

Hiroshi drifted back over to the shelves and scanned the paints. When he saw the jar of red powdered paint, he knew.

"I've got an idea." He grabbed a jar of black *sumi* ink and returned to the worktable. "Do you want to help?"

Skye shook her head and took a step back. "I didn't get any of the family art genes. I can't even draw a straight line."

"How about a circle?"

"Even worse. I'll just watch."

Hiroshi dipped his brush in the ink and painted a circle on the white *washi* paper. The ink would prevent the paint from bleeding outside of the circle. Next he opened the lid of the powered paint, added water, and stirred it. He tapped the brush three times on the edge of the jar and wiped the excess paint from the bristles, just as Grandfather used to do. He touched the brush to the *washi* paper and started filling in the circle, careful to keep the red paint inside the black line. Then he handed the brush to Skye.

"Here. You can fill in the rest of the circle if you want."

Skye looked unsure, but took the brush. "All I have to do is paint in the lines, right?"

Hiroshi nodded.

"But what if it drips outside the circle?"

"It won't if you tap the extra paint off, like this." He showed her

209

how to cradle the brush with a cupped hand to lead it from pot to kite.

Skye took a breath. "Here goes." She took so long to finish that Hiroshi thought the paint might dry on the brush. But finally it was done. He stood back to inspect their work—a single, red circle, just off-center. It was nothing like Grandfather's works of art, but it would have to do.

"It looks good," Skye said.

Hiroshi nodded. "The symbol of—"

"A winking dragon." Skye finished. She smiled. "No one else will guess—it's like a secret."

Hiroshi smiled, too. "A secret dragon." A secret dragon that Grandfather's spirit would surely recognize from the sky. At least Hiroshi hoped so.

Once the paint dried, it was time for a test run. As Hiroshi carried the winking dragon to the park, a light breeze tugged at the kite. He tightened his grip. The kite would have to be patient.

They reached the bottom of the hill, and Hiroshi paused, listening. "Not much wind today," he said. "I don't know if we can launch it." He eyed the lazy clouds overhead.

"Well." Skye shrugged. "There's only one way to find out."

When they reached the top of the hill, Hiroshi felt a whisper of a breeze. Closing his eyes, he concentrated on the feeble puffs of air and tried to read the direction of their path.

"So what do you think?" Skye asked. "Is it worth a try?"

Hiroshi nodded. "I think we can do it." He slipped the backpack off his shoulders and pulled out the reel.

Skye grinned. "This reel knows dragons."

Hiroshi nodded and fixed the line to the reel. "It will bring us luck—I just know it."

"I hope so." Skye took the kite and paced backward until they were several yards apart. She lifted the kite by the bridle.

As soon as Hiroshi felt a small gust of wind, he nodded. Skye released the kite, he ran with the line, and the winking dragon began its crooked climb.

Come on—go up! Fly! But he could see the breeze wasn't strong enough. The wind sighed as the kite drifted back down. Skye ran to catch it before it hit the ground. She shook her head as she walked it over.

"How many chances to launch will we get in the battle?" she asked.

"I'm not sure." Hiroshi shrugged. "Sometimes it takes a few tries."

Hiroshi studied the clouds that crept across the sky, sleepy and content. "There is some wind up there, but not much. Let's try again."

They set up the line and the kite once again. Hiroshi turned his back to the breeze. He unrolled some extra line, then held on with both hands.

"Now!"

Skye let go of the kite and Hiroshi pulled up on the line. The kite climbed higher and higher as Hiroshi shuffled backward, faster and faster. The wind took hold of the winking dragon, and Hiroshi let out more line, surrendering the kite to the sky.

"It worked!" Skye ran up, and Hiroshi grinned, handing her the reel. He grasped the line and practiced a few dives and twists with the kite before allowing it to drift even higher into the sky. Skye clapped and let out a whoop. Hiroshi laughed. They had done it. They'd made a kite that could fly.

But could it fight?

Walking across the wet grass of the National Mall, Skye willed her lunch to stay in her stomach. The Mall, a wide strip of grass, stretched from the steps of the US Capitol building all the way to the pencil-shaped Washington National Monument. Hundreds of kites in every color—some twice as big as Skye—flew near the base of the monument. Skye wanted to stay and see them all, but the *rokkaku* battle area was farther down the hill, and they still needed to register.

They started down the hill toward an area with white open tents, tables, and lines of people. Skye noticed that the nearby cherry trees had lost most of their petals and wondered if she'd have enough time to pluck a few and put them in her pocket for luck.

A loudspeaker announcement drifted across the field: "A brief pilots' meeting will begin in five minutes at the kite-hospital tent on the south side of the field."

The cherry blossoms would have to wait.

Skye and Hiroshi followed the signs for fliers while their parents wished them luck and headed for the spectator area. At the kite-hospital tent, Skye looked around at the competition. Old people, mostly—probably her parents' age. She didn't see any Japanese people, so she whispered to Hiroshi in Japanese: "What do you think?" She liked having a way to communicate without other people understanding—like a secret code.

Hiroshi looked around. "They'll have a lot of experience."

"Yeah, but so do you."

Hiroshi didn't look convinced. "No *washi*-paper kites."

He was right. All of the colorful six-sided kites were made of some nylon-looking material. Instead of bamboo, it looked like they had plastic tubing.

"Okay, time to begin." A man with a broad smile clapped his hands. He was wearing a baseball cap that said *National Cherry Blossom Kite Festival* and a matching sweatshirt. Cupping his hands around his mouth, he called, "Come on over, folks. We're ready to get started."

Skye spotted two girls heading their way. "Hey." She nudged Hiroshi. "They look our age."

Hiroshi turned. "You're right. They won't be experienced fliers."

The man in the cap went over the rules—lines no longer than fifty yards, gloves recommended, no intentional physical contact between contestants, three rounds of competition with ten minutes to repair kites in between.

Skye glanced at the sign that read *No Manja! No Cutting Line!* and she frowned.

"Good luck!" the man said. "Please check in with the registration tent and let them know you're here, and we'll be getting under way in about fifteen minutes." All the fliers headed toward the tent, and Skye and Hiroshi followed.

"Did you get all of that?" Skye asked as she filled out her registration form.

Hiroshi nodded. "I think so. It's the same as the rules back home."

213

"So why can't we cut lines? I thought we were supposed to. And do we need gloves? The guy said 'no intentional physical contact.' What if we bump into someone? Does that happen?" Skye's stomach felt like it was upside down, but Hiroshi seemed calm.

"*Manja* are cutting lines that have been coated in glass or metal so they cut better. We're allowed to cut other flier's lines, but we have to use regular line."

"Oh." That made sense. Running into a *manja* line sounded painful.

"And gloves—I never wear them. You'll have the reel, and I'll work the line with my hands. Some people wear gloves so their hands won't get cut."

"Regular line can cut you?"

Hiroshi shrugged. "Not if you're careful. Grandfather never wore gloves; he always said that if you can feel the line, it will tell you what to do."

Grandfather. *I don't know if you can see us, Grandfather, but we sure could use a little assistance today. Mostly it's me who needs help. But keep an eye on Hiroshi, too, just in case.*

"All fliers please report to the field," the loudspeaker announced.

"Wait," Skye said. "What about bumping into other people? Does that happen?

"It can. But it would mostly be me, since I'll be watching the kite, not where I'm going. Just follow me and let me know if I'm about to crash into anyone, okay? I'll let you know when I need more or less line."

"Okay. We can do this." Skye hoped she sounded more confident than she felt. She took one shaky breath, then followed the other fliers to the battle area.

214

The contestants all spread out inside the roped-off area. Skye counted twenty-two kites on the field. Most people wore gloves, but not the two girls she had seen earlier. She smiled and nodded their way, but they didn't smile back. Maybe they hadn't seen her. The reel in her hand felt warm compared to the cool spring air, and she wrapped her fingers around the handles.

Hiroshi inspected the winking dragon. When he looked at Skye, she gave him a thumbs-up. "We're ready," he said.

"Right," she answered, and looked at the sky, hoping for some sign that Grandfather was watching.

The voice over the loudspeaker brought Skye back down to earth. "Good luck, and may the best kite win!"

The spectators clapped, then the loudspeaker spat out one word: "Launch!" The fliers came to life, lifting their kites into the air.

At Hiroshi's nod, Skye let out the line. A second later Hiroshi stood facing the wind, holding the kite's bridle. He released it, and the winking dragon rose eagerly, climbing higher and higher. Skye backed up and let out more line.

"It's up! It's up!" Skye did a few hops, but Hiroshi kept his eyes on the kite as he grabbed the climbing dragon's line.

"Engage!" boomed the loudspeaker. The battle had begun.

Once the kite was up, Hiroshi felt like he could breathe. Here on the field the kites all spoke the same language. For the first time since moving to America, Hiroshi knew exactly what to do.

Although his focus was on the winking dragon, he could see Skye out of the corner of his eye. Grandfather had once told him that the one who controls the reel must stay invisible to the flier. He wished Grandfather had told Skye, too. At least now she'd stopped hopping around.

He caught sight of a black kite with a white star as it moved in closer to the winking dragon. Time to make a move.

"More line!"

In an instant he felt the slack as Skye let out the reel, and he was grateful for her quick response. The star kite hovered above the winking dragon before charging. Hiroshi pulled in his line, and the dragon rose up and away from danger. Calling for more line, he moved in, guiding his line closer and closer to the other kite's line. Contact! His hands tingled as the lines hummed. He pulled in his line, then let it out, repeating the motion until his line sawed through his opponent's with a snap. The black kite plummeted to earth like a shooting star. Its owner sprinted after it to begin repairs.

216

Skye was hopping again and whooping. Hiroshi grinned but didn't take his eyes off the dragon.

"Kite with flames behind you!" Skye called.

He whirled around to see a red kite with orange flames charging. Hiroshi moved in for the attack. He maneuvered the winking dragon until it floated level with the fire kite. The other flier knocked the winking dragon out of the way. The dragon fell a few yards, and Hiroshi heard Skye gasp.

"More line!"

Then a puff of wind scooped up the dragon, lifting it above the other kite. Hiroshi guided it closer and closer until it rammed the fire kite, sending it plunging to the ground. A crunching sound announced when it hit the grass. Another whoop from Skye, and more hopping.

Before Hiroshi could count how many kites remained, a plain blue kite the color of the sky slammed into the winking dragon. He called for more line and let the dragon fall, allowing it to find another gust of wind. Once it did he kept the dragon below the blue kite, then guided the line until his fingers told him the two lines had connected. He released some line, then pulled it in—release, pull, release, pull, release—until he lost track of where his hands ended and his line began. The blue kite tried to dodge out of the way, but the winking dragon stalked it relentlessly. Hiroshi played the line like a puppeteer until he saw the blue kite snap free—then twirl, flip, and spin toward the ground. Hiroshi was scanning the skies in search of the next kite when he heard applause from the crowd.

The last kite flying was the winking dragon.

Skye blinked in disbelief. Judging by the grin on Hiroshi's face, it must be true—the winking dragon had done it. They'd won the first round.

"Hiroshi! Skye!"

She waved at her parents, aunt, and uncle, who were cheering with the rest of the crowd. Hiroshi walked over as he started pulling the dragon back down, hand over hand.

"Nice job," he said.

"We did it!"

"The first round, yes."

Skye's fingers trembled as she rolled up the line. Something inside her hadn't expected them to really win. She looked up at the winking dragon, strutting like it knew it was in first place. Hiroshi had flown the kite like a champion. If Grandfather could see them from wherever he was, would he be proud of her, too?

Skye reeled in more line as the head judge came toward them with a huge grin. "Congratulations, you two! That was some fine flying you did out there."

"Thank you, sir." Hiroshi said. Skye thanked him, too, but she knew he was really there to congratulate Hiroshi.

The man turned to Skye. "Where did you kids get your kite?"

She nodded in Hiroshi's direction. "He made it."

"We made it," Hiroshi said, then turned his attention back to the kite and the line.

"Well, I helped." Skye smiled.

"Amazing. You don't see kites like that anymore." The judge shook his head. "Good luck in the next round." The judge walked off the field toward the kite hospital, where fliers raced around, trying to fix their kites in time for the next round. If the dragon crashed, would Hiroshi be able to fix it?

"Here it comes." Hiroshi had pulled the winking dragon low enough for Skye to reach it. "I've got it." Skye plucked the winking dragon from the air.

The girls with the sky-blue kite came back on the field and got ready for the next round, barely nodding at Hiroshi and Skye. "That blue kite has nothing on you," Skye whispered to the dragon. "Don't let it scare you."

As the other fliers rejoined them on the field, Skye checked the line. Her hands weren't shaking this time. Could they do it again? She counted only twelve teams on the field this time. It would be easier to move around with fewer people out there, but these were the twelve best teams.

Hiroshi held up the dragon and nodded. Skye gave him a thumbs-up.

"Launch!" commanded the loudspeaker. Hiroshi let go of the kite, and Skye hurried backward, letting the winking dragon climb. She held the reel steady while Hiroshi grabbed the line.

"Engage!"

The kites obeyed—crashing into each other and tangling lines. Skye shadowed Hiroshi as he moved across the field.

"Flier behind you, coming from your left," Skye said in Japanese. She figured now wasn't the time to confuse him with directions in English. As Hiroshi glanced over his shoulder, Skye spotted a hawk-faced kite moving in.

"On the dragon's right!" she called. Skye saw the hawk's line rub against theirs. The hawk's fierce eyes glared down at Skye. Those eyes reminded her of the dragon kite Grandfather had painted. She was mesmerized for a moment, then heard Hiroshi's call: "More line!"

Skye let the reel spin between her fingers. Out of the corner of her eye, she saw other kites tumbling and spiraling to the ground. Hiroshi was sawing his line against the hawk's line, but it was taking too long. The blue kite was coming in fast.

"Cut the line, Hiroshi!"

"I'm trying!" She could hear the frustration in his voice and wished she had a pair of scissors to cut the line herself.

But then the hawk's line snapped.

"Yes!" The hawk dove straight into the ground.

The blue kite swooped in, knocking the winking dragon aside. Skye didn't wait for Hiroshi's call; she let out more line and Hiroshi fed it to the dragon. When the dragon found another pocket of wind and steadied itself, Skye allowed herself to breathe. But when she saw Hiroshi moving the line back and forth, she realized that the lines had crossed.

Skye's heart felt like a bird in her rib cage trying to escape. She raced after Hiroshi as he ran, moving his line faster and faster.

And then the sky tipped and the grass rose up and Skye was on the ground. She felt the reel fly from her hand and saw it skitter after Hiroshi. He stopped and turned, but she waved him on.

"Go! I'm fine!" She scrambled to her feet. How could she have tripped? She raced after the reel, scooped it up, and caught up to Hiroshi. He was sawing the line back and forth, back and forth. Then his arms fell to his side and he lowered his head.

"What—?"

She watched helplessly as the line in Hiroshi's hand drifted down, kite-less. The winking dragon was falling, and Hiroshi took off after it. Skye heard the crowd's cheers. But this time they were clapping for the blue kite flying victorious overhead.

And it was all Skye's fault.

寬○

"Excuse me!"

Hiroshi leaped into the crowd, praying he wouldn't crash into anyone while keeping his eyes on the falling dragon. The wind didn't want to give up the kite; it rocked it back and forth, taunting Hiroshi. *Hurry up!* Hiroshi felt like shouting. They had less than ten minutes to make repairs before the championship round.

Finally the wind set the kite on the ground. Hiroshi held his breath while he checked for damage. The winking dragon was still in one piece. All the other kites in the battle had hit the ground at faster speeds. He knew the *washi* paper would not have survived that kind of crash. Was Grandfather's spirit watching over them after all?

Hiroshi sprinted toward the kite hospital, where Skye was waiting. Under the white tent, fliers cut lines and retied them. They ran their fingers over every bit of their sails, checking for rips.

"I'm so sorry." Skye took a shaky breath.

"It wasn't your fault." Hiroshi knew it wasn't. But if she hadn't have tripped, maybe . . . No use thinking about it now.

Skye looked like she was about to cry.

"Actually, I did something worse in a kite battle once."

Skye's face brightened. "Worse? Did you trip, too?"

222

"I didn't trip myself. I tripped Grandfather."

Skye's eyes grew wide. "You didn't!"

Hiroshi grinned. "I did. But he wasn't hurt, and he wasn't mad, and we won in the end."

Skye shook her head. "So maybe there's hope for us after all." She bent over the winking dragon to retie the line.

Hiroshi looked for the girls with the blue kite. He spotted them off behind the tents, kneeling on the grass.

Skye stood. "What are they up to?"

Hiroshi watched as the girls slipped their reel into a backpack and pulled out another one. Skye shrugged, turning her attention back to the winking dragon. Hiroshi was about to say it was time to go when something caught his eye.

"Skye, look." She turned, and Hiroshi nodded toward the girls.

"What is it?"

He switched to Japanese. "Were they wearing gloves before?"

Skye looked at the girls again and her eyes narrowed. "No, I don't think so. Why?"

"Because they just switched reels, and now they're wearing gloves. Something isn't right."

"But you said some people wear gloves. Most of the fliers last round had gloves on."

Hiroshi pointed to the sign: *No Manja! No Cutting Line!*

Skye gasped. "Do you really think—?"

Hiroshi put his finger to his lips. "It's hard to tell from here; the line doesn't look any different. But I won't know until I see it un-rolled."

"We have to tell someone! The judges should know about this."

"We can't—we don't have any proof."

"Well, when will you know for sure?"

The loudspeaker crackled, then a voice announced, "Fliers, five minutes to launch time."

Hiroshi's stomach flip-flopped as he picked up the winking dragon. "We have to go."

Skye grabbed the reel. "But won't it be obvious to the judges? If you can see the difference in their line, won't they be able to tell, too?"

Hiroshi thought for a moment and then relaxed. She had a point. "Unless—" he began.

"What? Unless what?"

Hiroshi looked back at the girls, but they seemed absorbed in inspecting their blue kite. "Unless they only coated it farther up, near the kite."

Skye nodded. "Then no one would know since that part would be way up in the sky."

"Except at launch time."

"Right. So you just get a look at the line when they launch, then if you see that it's coated, we tell the judges, and then they'll be out. We've already beaten the other kites, and we can do it again!" Skye smiled, like it would really be that easy.

"Even if I can see it up that close, there won't be time to tell the judges before the launch. And if we're wrong, we're out of the competition."

"Well, if they cut down our kite, we'll tell the judges then. After it's over. We'll win because they'll be disqualified."

Hiroshi frowned. "Then we'll look like sore losers. Besides, it would take us a few minutes to reach the judges and explain, giving the girls plenty of time to switch reels. It won't work, Skye."

224

"So what's the plan, then?"

"To win."

Hiroshi and Skye joined the fliers spread out on the field. Seven kites from the last round had been damaged beyond repair, leaving five teams now on the field.

"One minute to launch time."

Skye looked panicked. The girls with the blue kite had let out some line and looked ready to go.

Then Hiroshi had an idea. He handed the winking dragon to Skye. "Here, hold this. I'm going to wish them luck."

Skye looked surprised and then grinned. "Nice plan."

Hiroshi jogged over to where the girls stood, well away from the other fliers. The one holding the kite made a move as if she wanted to hide the kite behind her back. Instead she handed it to her partner and stepped forward. She did not look pleased.

"Thirty seconds to launch time," the loudspeaker announced.

"I wanted to wish you luck." Hiroshi held out his hand.

The girl looked wary. She stuck out her hand and shook his. "Yeah, um, good luck."

He offered his hand to the other girl. She had to shift the kite to the other hand to shake his, and that's when he saw it: the glint off the section of the line nearest the kite.

It was coated.

He didn't let his gaze rest on the line more than half a second. He shook her hand, then jogged back to Skye.

"Ten seconds!"

"Hiroshi!" Skye squeaked and handed him the kite, her line already unrolled for the launch.

Hiroshi nodded. "It's *manja*, up at the top."

225

"Launch!"

Hiroshi ran with the winking dragon, and up it went, anxious to begin.

"What do we do?" Skye's voice came from beside him.

"We have to knock it from the sky. We can't let their line touch ours, because I'm not sure how far down the coating runs."

"Maybe one of the other kites will knock it down first."

Hiroshi doubted it, but before he had a chance to say so, he saw the hawk kite hovering near the winking dragon. He didn't hesitate. With a few tugs of his line, he guided the winking dragon closer and closer. As soon as he felt his line cross the hawk's line, he began sawing, faster and faster, until he felt the break. The hawk sailed to the ground, a tendril of cut line trailing behind it like a tail.

"On your left."

Hiroshi spotted the lightning-bolt kite just as it snapped the line of another kite. Before the lightning bolt's flier had time to savor the victory, the winking dragon knocked it to the side, pushing it downward. But the lightning bolt recovered, and Hiroshi's hands hummed when the lines crossed. He immediately pulled in some line, then released it. Pull, release, pull, release as the lines rubbed against each other. His opponent did the same, but Hiroshi moved faster. Within a few minutes Hiroshi felt the familiar snap as the lightning bolt headed straight for the ground.

He looked for the next kite. For a moment he didn't see any others. Where was the blue kite?

"Behind you, Hiroshi!"

Hiroshi had almost mistaken it for a piece of sky.

"This is it, Hiroshi!" Skye called. Hiroshi nodded. This was their chance.

Keeping his eyes on his line, Hiroshi guided the winking dragon closer to the blue kite. The cheers and the announcer's voice grew louder and louder, buoying the kites as they shot higher into the sky. The blue kite raced ahead, then stalled and dropped below the dragon. Its line rubbed against the dragon's line, but only for a moment. Hiroshi broke contact and led the winking dragon out of danger.

The blue kite hit a spot of windless sky and began to drop. The girl let out more line, allowing the kite to find the wind, giving Hiroshi a few seconds to think.

What would Grandfather do?

Read the wind, that's what he'd do. Hiroshi had been so focused on the blue kite that he hadn't been paying attention to the wind.

He heard a thud followed by Skye's voice saying, "Hey! Watch where you're going!" When he turned, Skye was on the ground, the reel holder from the other team helping her up. Skye scowled. "You did that on purpose!"

The other girl grinned. "Maybe." The judges were too far away to hear. The girl helped Skye up—probably to make it look like it'd been an accident.

Hiroshi was about to ask Skye if she was okay when her mouth opened and she pointed. "Look out!"

He felt it before he saw it. His line buzzed with the friction from the other line as they crossed. Hiroshi led the winking dragon away, pulling it lower than the blue kite. He knew the blue kite would come after him, and it did. As the blue kite crept lower, Hiroshi forced himself to be patient. *Just wait for it; let it come to you.*

The two lines formed a triangle with the ground, and the gap between the kites was closing at the top. A little bit more . . .

When the blue kite was almost on top of the winking dragon, Hiroshi let the line go. The winking dragon shot up, slamming into a corner of the blue kite like an uppercut punch. The blue kite tipped and spun and headed straight for the ground. The girls began to shout something and tried unwinding their reel, letting out more line, their hands a blur. Their kite finally found a low spot in the sky where it hovered.

Hiroshi raced in the direction of the girls, Skye at his side.

"We're going to cut the line."

"What?" Skye sounded horrified. "But the coating—"

"Is up at the top. They're focused on getting their kite back up. We'll slice the line down low."

Hiroshi pulled on his line, leading it to the blue kite's line. When the blue kite started to climb, the lines clashed. As soon as he felt the tingle, Hiroshi started sawing the line back and forth, back and forth.

"No! He's too low on the line!" one girl shouted to the other. Hiroshi understood her words. His arms burned, but he couldn't stop now. Within a few seconds he felt the pop of the line. His heart flew as the blue kite flipped and fluttered its way out of the sky, and the crowd roared its approval.

The winking dragon had won.

Hiroshi and Sorano

Hiroshi and Skye stood in the middle of the field, stunned. Their parents rushed over, talking and smiling and hugging all at once. Skye and Hiroshi grinned at each other.

"Excuse me, may I have a word with the winners?" someone said.

"Do you mind if we snap a quick photo?" said another. Hiroshi and Skye turned to see a group with badges that read *Press Pass*.

One man stepped forward. "I'm with the *Washington Post*. I'd love to get a photo of you two for our online Metro section."

Skye and Hiroshi looked at their parents, who nodded their approval. The reporter backed up and focused his camera lens while others did the same.

"Which camera are we supposed to look at?" Skye said out of the side of her mouth.

"I'm not sure," Hiroshi whispered back.

A woman gestured to Hiroshi. "Do you mind holding the kite up a bit more?" Hiroshi raised the kite, Skye held up the reel, and the cameras all seemed to go off at once.

"The judge said this kite is one-of-a-kind," one reporter said. "Can you tell us a little about it?"

Before either Hiroshi or Skye could answer, a smiling man came up from behind them, holding two shiny trophies. He

229

stepped in front of the reporters. "Ladies and gentlemen, I am Mr. Takumi Sato, president of the National Cherry Blossom Festival. I would like to be among the first to congratulate our winners today." The reporters tucked their notebooks under their arms and clapped along with the crowd that had gathered around them.

Mr. Sato turned to Hiroshi. "*Omedetou gozaimasu.*" He then turned to Skye and repeated in English: "Congratulations."

Skye bowed. "*Arigato gozaimasu,* Sato-san."

"Yes, thank you, Mr. Sato," Hiroshi added in English.

Mr. Sato looked from Hiroshi to Skye, then back again. "I apologize to you both." He looked at Hiroshi. "Your registration form was filled out in Japanese"—he turned to Skye—"and yours in English."

Hiroshi and Skye looked at each other and laughed.

"Actually, we both speak Japanese and English," Skye said.

One of the reporters stepped forward. "I heard you two made this kite. Is that correct?"

Skye looked at Hiroshi and he smiled. "Yes, we did," she said.

"It's made of *washi* paper and bamboo," Hiroshi added.

Mr. Sato sighed. "It reminds me of the kites I flew when I was young. May I?" He held out his hand, and Hiroshi gave him the winking dragon. "This is exquisite."

Hiroshi nodded. "Thank you, sir."

"One more clarification," a reporter said. "I want to make sure I'm getting your names right for the article. You both have the last name Tsuki, correct?"

Skye and Hiroshi nodded.

"And your first names are Skye and Hiroshi?"

Hiroshi nodded. But Skye stepped forward. "My first name is

actually Sorano. S-o-r-a-n-o." Hiroshi looked at her. She shrugged and grinned.

The reporters packed away their cameras and started to walk away. "Oh, look!" someone called.

Suddenly the air seemed filled with cherry blossom petals swirling and dancing on the wind. Skye drew in a breath. A reporter unzipped his camera bag. "I didn't think there were enough blossoms left on those trees for this kind of thing."

"They're beautiful," someone else said.

Skye closed her eyes and felt the strong, fragile blossoms whisper around her. And she knew.

Hiroshi hardly noticed the blossoms, but he did feel the wind shift. Like always, he paused and looked skyward to see what the breeze would do next. And that's when he saw it. Floating overhead was a single cloud the color of a white kimono. Hiroshi could make out the winding tail, long body, and head. He blinked again.

A dragon cloud. He remembered what Grandfather had said that day on the hill. *The dragon is a creature of the sea. When it takes to the sky, it means it is looking for something precious it has lost. When it finds what it was looking for, it returns to the sea in the form of rain.*

The first gentle raindrops fell on Hiroshi's upturned face. And he knew.

Hiroshi and Sorano turned back for a last glimpse of the competition field. People trickled up the hill toward the kite show at the Washington Monument. One of the white tents was being taken down, billowing sails against spring-green grass.

They watched the wind lead the dragon cloud and the cherry blossoms eastward. Hiroshi and Sorano knew they'd be back.

Acknowledgments

This story never would have taken flight without many helping hands.

For the bamboo bones that make the story fly straight and true, I thank Harold Ames, past (and likely future) winner of the National Cherry Blossom Kite Festival *Rokkaku* Challenge in Washington, DC, and David Gomberg of Gomberg Kite Productions, International. Two teachers in the Japanese Partial Immersion Program in Fairfax County, Virginia, checked my manuscript for cultural and linguistic accuracy. *Domo arigato gozaimasu* to Akiko Bentz of Great Falls Elementary and Yuko Frost of Fox Mill Elementary. Thanks to ABGC Cheetahs and the X-treme 98 Red girls' soccer team for teaching me all I know about soccer.

For the *washi* paper that takes ages to create, but is beautiful and strong, heartfelt thanks to the communities of writers I've had the privilege of knowing over the years: Verla Kay's Blueboards, the Gango, and the Lit Wits, my critique partners extraordinaire— Cynthia Jaynes Omololu, Ammi-Joan Paquette, Julie Phillipps, and Kip Wilson—whose invaluable feedback helped shape this story and whose friendship and support helped shape me as a writer.

For the painted colors that are the finishing touches to this story, my respect and thanks to my agent, Erin Murphy, and my

232

editor, Emily Mitchell, both of whom are smart, savvy, and funny. And to illustrator Kelly Murphy, a thousand thanks for bringing my characters and setting to life on the cover—Grandfather would be impressed.

For the reel and line that both let me fly and keep me grounded, love and thanks to my family. My parents, Chuck and Carol Dias, read several versions of the manuscript, offered their feedback, and never stopped believing. My children, Teah, Sofia, and Jordan, let their mom spend oodles of time on the computer and gave their kid stamp of approval as the story progressed.

And finally for the wind, Davide, who makes my heart soar.